PRAISE FOR
madeleine is sleeping

A National Book Award Finalist
A New York Public Library Young Lions Fiction Award Finalist
A *Washington Post Book World* Best Book of the Year
A *Publishers Weekly* Best Book of the Year

"A dream of a book: mysterious, funny, and startlingly beautiful.
If we had begun to suspect that American novelists had abandoned
their grand and reckless ambitions, here is Sarah Shun-lien Bynum
to give us hope."
— Michael Cunningham, author of *The Hours* and *Specimen Days*

"This is buoyant, intriguing, lovely, and sui generis. There is much
to admire—inventiveness, fine detail, historical allusions that have
a pleasing resonance and grace about them. Legerdemain is always
a thing to be respected in writing, and in this book, its charms are
manifest."
— Marilynne Robinson, author of *Housekeeping* and *Gilead*

"This was as exciting a story as I remember anyone showing me for
years—fresh, imaginative, original, and beautiful."
— Stuart Dybek, author of *I Sailed with Magellan*

"Luminous . . . Bynum's lush, poetic imagery is full of vivid,
sensuous details one can almost smell, taste, and feel . . . The most
compelling through-line is the sexual awakening of Madeleine . . .

It culminates in a moment of pure physical need and awareness that the author beautifully captures with a reflection that is achingly human and poignantly telling."
—*The Boston Globe*

"Audacious in form and content . . . Like a dream, this novel fills the mind with tantalizing ambiguity, haunting images, and innocent longings that are slow to fade."
—*The Christian Science Monitor*

"Hypnotic . . . *Madeleine Is Sleeping* tiptoes the line between fantasy and reality, between history and myth. It gently suspends the reader in the comfortable twilight moment that comes just before falling asleep. By blurring those distinctions, Bynum makes readers question the extent to which we may be sleepwalking through our lives. And she asks us to discover what our own dreams can teach us. The result is a small, enchanting novel that appeals to the naughty, insolent child in each of us."
—*USA Today*

"Delicate, grave and almost evanescent . . . The masterful way [Bynum] has kept her disappearing balls in the air—mostly by means of a voice at once sensuous and humorous, mellifluous and matter-of-fact—reminds of no one, unless it's that wonderful dream-narrator we all possess, who tells us the most outlandish and dirty stories quite calmly, and doesn't mind doubling us and others, or making things happen twice at the same time."
—*The Washington Post Book World*

"In Bynum's luminous and daring novel, the border between dreams and waking is not so much blurred as erased: Each delicious chapter is like a half-remembered episode from the depths of sleep, as indelible as it is fleeting."
—*Los Angeles Times Book Review*

"Deciding what is and isn't the stuff of dreams is half the fun in this magical, circuitous tale . . . Madeleine's past, present and future unfold in short, lyrical, self-contained chapters that flirt between fantasy and reality in charming, matter-of-fact prose, equal parts delightful, intriguing and confusing."
—*Time Out New York*

"Bynum's voice is vivid, her use of language incisive and surprising. Perhaps the best thing that can happen in a first novel is just this: that it be unquestionably interesting, that it dare something, and that it leave much to be said. Then the writer has truly set out on her path."
—*Bookforum*

"Bynum's lush, mesmerizing sentences pull readers into a circular narrative populated by fantastical characters right out of Alice's Wonderland."
—*The Boston Phoenix*

"In this lush, earthy and erotic story, the title character, Madeleine, is one part child, one part adventuress and one part adult . . . The story is captivating, as is the form of the book . . . A fascinating adventure—one the average reader isn't likely to forget anytime soon."

—*The Capital Times* (Madison, WI)

"Replete with Kafkaesque metamorphoses, Freudian fantasies, Aesopian justice and religious metaphor, the novel is equal parts fairy tale, fable, romance and bildungsroman . . . [Those] looking for a challenging, unusual read will be thrilled by the imagination and mysterious energy that haunt this remarkable debut."

—*Publishers Weekly* (starred review)

"[Bynum] crafts this wicked little lullaby with the poise of a master. You might find this little tale invading your Circadian rhythms at night."

—*Philadelphia Weekly*

"Bynum has tapped into the great unconscious, mined the vast pool of imagination and prepared a feast of the exotic, the erotic and the forbidden. Carefully incised, the human heart is revealed: the fragile chambers, the connections, the fumbling toward acceptance and understanding."

—curledup.com

"The book taps in to what is wonderful about reading . . . Virtually every page pops with an arresting sentence, a vivid image, or an entire paragraph of plot that you simply have to read again because you don't believe [Bynum] just said what you thought she said."

—*Conversational Reading*

madeleine is
sleeping

SARAH SHUN-LIEN BYNUM

madeleine is sleeping

A HARVEST BOOK
HARCOURT, INC.
Orlando Austin New York San Diego Toronto London

Requests for permission to make copies of any part of the work should
be mailed to the following address: Permissions Department, Harcourt, Inc.,
6277 Sea Harbor Drive, Orlando, Florida 32887-6777.

www.HarcourtBooks.com

The Library of Congress has cataloged the hardcover edition as follows:
Bynum, Sarah Shun-lien.
Madeleine is sleeping/Sarah Shun-lien Bynum.
p.   cm.
1. Young women—Fiction.   2. Triangles (Interpersonal relations)—Fiction
3. Circus performers—Fiction.   4. Romanies—Fiction.   5. Villages—Fiction.
6. Dreams—Fiction.   7. France—Fiction.   8. Sleep—Fiction.
I. Title.
PS3602.Y58M33   2004
813'.6—dc22   2004005224
ISBN-13: 978-0151-01059-2   ISBN-10: 0-15-101059-5
ISBN-13: 978-0156-03227-8 (pbk.)   ISBN-10: 0-15-603227-9 (pbk.)

Text set in Adobe Garamond
Designed by Linda Lockowitz

Printed in the United States of America

First Harvest edition 2005
A C E G I K J H F D B

For Mama and Papa

madeleine is
sleeping

hush

HUSH, MOTHER SAYS. Madeleine is sleeping. She is so beautiful when she sleeps, I do not want to wake her.

The small sisters and brothers creep about the bed, their gestures of silence becoming magnified and languorous, fingers floating to pursed lips, tip toes rising and descending as if weightless. Circling about her bed, their frantic activity slows; they are like tiny insects suspended in sap, kicking dreamily before they crystallize into amber. Together they inhale softly and the room fills with one endless exhalation of breath: Shhhhhhhhhhhhh.

madeleine dreams

A GROTESQUELY FAT WOMAN lives in the farthest corner of the
village. Her name is Matilde. When she walks to market, she must
gather up her fat just as another woman gathers up her skirts,
daintily pinching it between her fingers and hooking it over her
wrists. Matilde's fat moves about her gracefully, sighing and rustling
with her every gesture. She walks as if enveloped by a dense storm
cloud, from which the real, sylph-like Matilde is waiting to emerge,
blinding as a sunbeam.

mme. cochon

ON MARKET DAY, children linger in their doorways. They hide tight, bulging fists behind their backs and underneath their aprons. When Matilde sweeps by, trailing her luxurious rolls of fat behind her, the children shower her. They fling bits of lard, the buttery residue scraped from inside a mother's churn, the gristle from Sunday dinner's lamb. The small fistfuls have grown warm and slippery from the children's kneading, and the air is rich with a comforting, slightly rancid smell.

Mme. Cochon, are you hungry? they whisper as she glides by.

Matilde thinks she hears curiosity in their voices. She smiles mildly as she continues on, dodging the dogs that have run out onto the street, snuffling at the scraps. It feels, somehow, like a parade. It feels like a celebration.

surprise

ONCE, AS MATILDE made her way through the falling fat, she was startled by a peculiar but not unpleasant throb, which originated in her left shoulder but soon travelled clockwise to the three other corners of her broad back. She wondered if the children were now hurling soup bones, and made an effort to move more swiftly, but suddenly the joyous barrage slowed to a halt. The children stood absolutely still, lips parted, yellow butter dripping onto their shoes. They stared at her with a curiosity Matilde did not recognize.

Hearing a restless fluttering behind her, she twisted about and glimpsed the frayed edges of an iridescent wing. With great caution, she flexed her meaty shoulder blades and to her delight, the wing flapped gaily in response. Matilde had, indeed, fledged two pairs of flimsy wings, the lower pair, folded sleekly about the base of her spine, serving as auxiliary to the grander ones above.

flight

LEAPING CLUMSILY, all four wings flapping, her fat, like sandbags,
threatening to ground her, Matilde greets the air with arms spread
wide open. A puff of wind lifts the hem of her skirts, seems to tickle
her feet, and Matilde demands, Up, up, up! With a groan, the wind
harnesses Matilde's impressive buttocks and dangles her above the
cobblestones, above the hungry dogs, above the dirty children with
fat melting in their fists.

stirring

MADELEINE STIRS in her sleep.

hush

WHEN MADELEINE SLEEPS, Mother says, the cows give double their milk. Pansies sprout up between the floorboards. Your father loves me, but I remain slender and childless. I can hear the tumult of pears and apples falling from the trees like rain.

Smooth your sister's coverlet. Arrange her hair on the pillowcase. Be silent as saints. We do not wish to wake her.

madeleine dreams

ON DARK MORNINGS, when the church still lay in shadow, Saint Michel looked absent-minded, forlorn, penned in by the lead panes that outlined the sad slope of his jaw. She thought him by far the most heartbreaking of the saints, and occasionally yearned to squeeze the long, waxen fingers that were pressed together so impassibly as they pointed towards heaven.

He had been a prince once, whose appetite was such that he could never quite keep his mouth closed. In defiance of medieval conventions, even his portraits attest to his hunger: his lips are always ajar, teeth wetly bared, as if about to bite into his tenants' capons or cheeses or one of their firm daughters. In his castle's feasting hall, he liked to stage elaborate tableaux vivants, resurrecting the classical friezes he had seen in his travels, himself always cast as the hero or the young god, a bevy of peasant girls enlisted as dryads, pheasants and rank trout imitating eagles and dolphins. Imagine the depravity, the priest whispers: women with nipples as large and purple as plums, birds molting, dead fish suspended from the rafters, and rising in the midst of them all, the achingly glorious Michel, oblivious to the chaos surrounding him. His vanity was unmatched!

penitence

AND THEN A PLAGUE STRUCK, a drought descended, and Michel found God.

While outside his castle walls the pestilence raged, Michel was struck by the face of the crucified Lord, preserved in a primitive icon that hung beneath the stairs. His fair face had been obliterated by tears and blood; His perfect body was desiccated and dotted with flies. Wracked by self-reproach, the prince vowed to destroy his own beauty; he surrendered himself and his lands to the monastery at Rievaulx, where he spent the rest of his days inflicting torture upon himself.

He suffered through flagellations, hair shirts, and fasting while the abbot meticulously chronicled his decline: Prince Michel can barely leave his pallet; his flesh has fallen away; repeated flaying has reopened and infected old wounds; his sackcloth has spawned monstrous lesions about his groin. It was as Michel wished. When he finally expired, his face was contorted in anguish, his loveliness effaced by tears and blood. The abbot washed the ravaged body and laid it upon its bier, but by morning the saint had been miraculously restored to perfection, his body whole and sound, his face flawless and somber. This is the Saint Michel depicted in the cathedral window. Even the devout find it difficult to remember the suffering he endured.

I should have loved him more, she thought, if he had remained mutilated.

recognition

ON A SUNDAY IN SUMMER, a blade of empyreal light illuminated his once melancholy face, and she instantly recognized it as her own. Why, it's me, she said to herself, without wonder. I have been looking at myself all along.

And the face was no longer lengthened in sorrow, but bright and fluid with color. She stood up from her family's pew and walked towards the stained glass, her eyes locked with her own. At the altar, she pivoted on her toes and faced the congregation. Look upon me, she said.

Stepping down from the altar, she approached a stout man sitting in the front pew, the collection plate balanced on his knees, and she touched his chest, with all the tenderness in the world. His stiff Sunday vest peeled away like an orange rind, and she grazed her fingertips against the polished, orderly bones of his rib cage. Beneath, she found a curled and pulsing bud, and when she blew on it, it began to unfurl its sanguine petals, one by one. His heart unfolded before her.

She worked her way down each pew, gently touching and blowing as she went, and when she looked around she noticed, with pleasure, that the small flowers she had uncovered were of a heliotropic variety; their delicate heads nodded to her wherever she went, following her movements like those of the sun.

animals

THE SMALL, PLIANT SIBLINGS heed Mother's bidding. Among the morning chores is the task that gives them most delight. First, you must sweep the walkway. After that, you must kiss grandmother's forehead. You must also lug empty pails to where Papa is milking. Only then are you entrusted with Mother's heirloom, a hand mirror whose face you hold out to the morning air like a butterfly net, catching the chill in midflight.

Madeleine is as still as a mummy, but when they hold the mirror beneath her nose, ghostly shapes appear on its cold surface. The children shove to see the results. A rabbit! Madeleine exhales again: an anteater! A menagerie of vaporous animals escapes from her nostrils and instantly disappears: the mirror records and erases in the same moment. Jean-Luc captures a whale. Claude, a pregnant sow. Beatrice says that she sees only cows.

Do not worry, Maman. Madeleine is still sleeping.

she dreams

WHEN M. MARAIS ordered a new viol, he requested that the
instrument's head be fashioned after the face of his neighbor's
youngest daughter, Charlotte. She sat diligently before the master
craftsman as he whittled away her likeness, until M. Marais was
pleased with the result and announced the portrait complete.

With the beautiful viol nestled between his thighs, he drew
the bow across the strings.

It is as if you were singing, he told the girl. This is how I
imagine your voice.

That is not me, Charlotte declared. That is only my face.
I think I will name her Griselda.

From then on, whenever she heard the moan of the viol,
Charlotte would trot next door and say hello to her face. Allo,
Griselda! she would exclaim, putting M. Marais terribly out of
sorts.

the marriage

AS SOON AS CHARLOTTE was confirmed, M. Marais visited her father and asked for her hand in marriage. Although the father argued persuasively in favor of Charlotte's several older sisters, praising one's graceful figure, another's delicate needlework, another's splendid hair, the acclaimed musician would accept none other than Charlotte herself. So the father relinquished her, ruefully, for she was his favorite and he had hoped to spend his old age watching her bloom into womanhood.

consummation

AT THE NUPTIAL HOUR, the servants passed through Charlotte as if she were a shade, a ghostly emanation of her corporeal groom. For the ceremony, attended only by the master craftsman and her regretful father, she had been dressed in filmy white. She had reflected, like the moon, M. Marais's bulky and brilliant mass of figured silks, brocades, velvets, rocaille lace. Now, wandering alone through the corridors, she stopped a scullery maid and begged directions to the bridal chamber.

The oaken door sighed like the entrance to a vault.

Quick, quick! These garters are insufferable!

Through the crack, she could see a naked sliver of M. Marais, flanked by two menservants he was swatting about the head. It's me, Charlotte, she announced through the opening. How strange it sounded finally to say it.

The musician shrieked and clutched himself, girlishly modest, trying to conceal both his breasts and his groin. Go away! he exclaimed, like a woman shooing hens. Go away this instant!

Charlotte hurriedly shut the door and skittered back a few paces: she imagined that she should feel relief but instead was experiencing a peculiar sense of disappointment. Glancing down, she saw the gaping keyhole. It winked at her, wisely, like a friend. Charlotte knelt, and looked inside.

The keyhole was like a telescope, unfolding before her the lush landscape of M. Marais's body. She spied his mossy buttocks, their dark and moist ravine; his nipples peeking out from his breasts, like two rosy cherubs in a cumulus cloud. The menservants had stripped him down to an exoskeleton of garters and restraints, but the more clothes he shed, the less naked he seemed, as if his flesh, freed from its constricting network of laces and stays, could finally embrace him in all its splendor. He stroked his voluptuous stomach and then settled himself, purring, onto the enormous bed. It groaned rapturously beneath him.

Unseen, Charlotte's bright brown eye flickered in the keyhole, wet with pity and desire, guttering like a candle.

her wish

CLOISTERED IN M. MARAIS'S ESTATE, Charlotte grew lonely and wistful and depended more and more upon the companionship of her face, Griselda. When the violist took his afternoon nap, Charlotte would steal into his practice rooms and carefully lay the instrument down on its back. Stretching out beside it, she would slide her hands up and down the supine viol, delighting in its smooth expanses and the seven strings that hovered tautly down its spine. As she traced the fingers of her right hand up and down the viol's strings, she would, with her left hand, mirror the same movement along her own body, trailing her fingernails from her chin to her mons.

I wish, she said to Griselda, that I had strings too.

hirsute

AS THE LONELY DAYS PASSED, Charlotte silently watched her body sprout resilient black hairs. At first it seemed as if only her brush of pubic hair had run amok, scaling up her stomach like a vine, but one morning, while reading an epistolary novel, she rested a bristling chin on her palm and realized that Griselda was granting her secret wish. By that evening, a dense, furry trail was already creeping up her décolletage.

M. Marais, squinting across the lengthy dinner table, was dismayed.

inscription

THE MUSICIAN methodically withdrew the carving knife from where it burrowed in the turkey's haunches, which sputtered in protest as he pulled it out. Rising with a sigh, he trundled down the length of the dinner table, and the room seemed to quiver with his seismic grace. The knife dripped fowl juices onto the tiles, leaving a trail of congealing fat as if M. Marais, like Hansel lost in the woods, might need to find his way back to his seat. Charlotte panted softly. My husband will slice me open, she told herself. And she imagined two identical wounds—the *f*-holes, the chiseled curves out of which the viol cries—inscribed in her own torso, curling up from her pelvic bones like a sly smile. Her network of organs and intestines would be pinkly exposed, like the wonderful wax anatomical woman she had seen last year at the fair. Charlotte's fingers began to scrabble at her laces.

She could smell M. Marais as he drew nearer—the fermenting scent of the enormously fat—and she bared her stomach, resplendent with black and horse-like hairs. But when her husband seized her, he gripped only her chin, tilting it in the air, maneuvering her head this way and that, and eyed her with the patience of a portraitist. Then the carving knife scraped down her gullet, and she watched as the shorn hair fell into her lap, plummeting in quick, sad clumps like lead-filled pigeons from the sky.

relic

AFTER DINNER, the musician retired and Charlotte, as was her habit, sneaked into Griselda's chambers. The lovely viol languished by the windowsill, and Charlotte crept up on her from behind, her silver sewing scissors glinting in the starlight. When she snipped the lowest string, it protested plaintively, but as she severed one after another, the twanging grew hysterical and shrill. Forgive me, Charlotte wept, winding each newly cut string around her wrist. I only want a memento.

She shed her filmy gown and rent it into shreds, which she spun into a filament as fine and strong as gossamer. And she lowered herself, spider-like, down the estate wall, with Griselda braced against the open window to anchor her. When her feet tickled the shrubbery, she looked up once more at the shorn viol, then she fled into the night, stark naked and stubbled.

fruit

PAPA GROWS IMPATIENT with the fruit that litters his orchard. The air assumes the rich rot of a winery; he complains that breathing alone will make him drunk. In the evening the children wander home, bloated and sticky, but still they cannot eat the pears as quickly as they fall. The local birds, too, are so fat with apple that they can barely reach their roosts at night, and when darkness falls, the orchard floor bubbles as the sated birds make listless, halfhearted efforts at flight.

preserves

MOTHER DECIDES ON tarts and preserves. She hugs a cast iron cauldron to her belly and tells her children to feed its hungry gape.

There will be apple butter for daily use. Fine pear jelly for holidays. Tartes aux pommes for neighbors who have been unusually kind.

stirring

MADELEINE STIRS in her sleep.

she dreams

MARGUERITE SINGS THE HERO. In Venice and in Mantua. Breasts tamed by wide strips of muslin, a dulled sword rubbing warmly against her gams, she inspires in the composer his most fearsome arias. The tortured Radamisto, spying his wife's fine white hand as it disappears beneath the currents. Sextus, hot with youth and vengeance, pleading with the shade of his murdered father. And brave blustering Tauris, defiant Tauris, the general who alone dares Theseus to battle. She sings them in Bologna and Reggio, in Milan, Parma, Naples, Florence. In London and in Versailles. She is adulated. George I and the Princess Royal stand godparents, by proxy, to the daughter who had strained, unforgiving, against the buttons of Tauris's starched uniform.

Marguerite is the primo uomo. She is the leading man.

impostor

UNTIL THE ARRIVAL of an impostor whose very unnaturalness makes him all the more irresistible. Senesino, the celebrated castrato. A curious aberration. Even an abomination. Indeed, he is illegal: against the law of God. How wicked that Rome, the fulcrum of excommunication, should be the home of the castrati. The city hides them away in its bowels, together with the whores and the Protestants, but if tenacious, one will find several there. In the Conservatorios they lie upstairs, by themselves, in warmer compartments than the other boys, for fear of colds. Influenzas. Inflammations. In the smallest hours of the night, the masters comb the sleeping quarters. A tender foot, which has twitched free from the bed linens, shadowkicking in dreamy repetition the demonic barn cat it remembers from home: this hot, tender foot is coveted, tucked jealously back beneath the counterpane. An acute sensitivity to boyish sniffles makes the conservatory staff anxious and high-strung. Colds might not only render the fragile voices unfit at present, but hazard the entire loss of them forever. And what a loss. These are the voices of angels.

surgery

THE COMPOSER discovered Senesino in the company of the Duke
of Wurtemburg, whose retinue includes twenty ballet dancers, three
trained monkeys, a small string orchestra, fifteen castrati, and two
surgeons from Bologna. The two treat their operation with the
strictest professionalism: they wield their instruments only on the
condition that the young subject has been tried as to the probability
of the voice. The boy muffled, the heady reek of ether, the surgeon
delicately sweating, and brava! The vas deferens is severed. Nothing
now will touch the resonant high C; the vein is closed down, like a
mine. Senesino's mother, it is rumored, keeps the dainty pair
pickled in a tiny clay pot.

The boy ages into a fleshy and strangely hairless man.

menses

ONCE DETHRONED, Marguerite is bitter.

A vocal absurdity, she sniffs. He is nothing but a caged nightingale!

But the composer remains unmoved. He has made his decision. The dark-hued female alto, fragrant and soiled, is not the voice of a hero. But Senesino! Such purity. Such extraordinary range. Lily-white, crystalline, without stain.

The stain, Marguerite grumbles, of my menstrual blood.

adieus

AS SHE BIDS HER FAREWELLS from the stage, Marguerite curtsies to the gelding. She reprises a couplet that a poet of great celebrity has penned for the occasion:

But let old charmers yield to new;
Happy soil, adieu! adieu!

The audience murmurs at her pretty sportsmanship. They crane to examine the castrato, who is perched in the composer's private box, shielding his smile with a gloved and demure hand. He whispers in the composer's ear, promising, Together we will delight them.

The composer, prompted, flatters the castrato, but he is interrupted: My timbre is flawless, yes. But it is the cruelty of my condition that will afford them such unbearable pleasures.

Marguerite, suddenly immodest, makes a rude gesture from the stage. She grabs her genitals lovingly. She flicks her hand from beneath her chin. Her wrist snaps in the air with wonderful elasticity.

success

MOTHER IS FLUSHED with business. Her preserves fetch an admirable price. Visitors arrive from long distances, grown ravenous and dissatisfied from the stories they have heard. I will not be happy, a dying girl says, if I cannot taste those heavenly preserves. In the city, Mother is told, the rich have made a habit of spreading it on their morning rolls.

Mother is always distracted, floured, clotted with fruit meat. She bobs up from her cauldron, dabs her upper lip, and asks the small children: Is Madeleine too hot?

They flank the bed and roll up their sleeves as they have seen the midwife do. Small hands press expertly against her throat, her cheeks, her eyelids. Madeleine is snowy beneath their fingertips. But is she perhaps a little warm right here, by her left temple? We had better feel once more. To be safe.

prince

A HANDSOME MAN appears at the door, wearing a bristling
moustache. He is not craving preserves. He is asking for Madeleine.
    Claude says, She is sleeping.
    The handsome man answers, I have come to awaken her.
    Claude asks, How are you going to do that?
    I am going to kiss her mouth.
    Wait a minute.

    Claude shuts the door.

princess

MOTHER'S FINGERS TWITCH as she makes her calculations. Into the tub they bathe in on Saturdays, she stirs enough ingredients for one hundred tarts. Four sacks of flour, a winter's worth of lard. Begrudgingly, a fistful of salt.

Mother kneads the face. Jean-Luc, the legs. Beatrice dimples the torso. And Mimi, the youngest, shapes the two lush arms.

Her body grows golden with an egg yolk glaze.

Papa's woolen nightcap goes on last.

Suddenly, Mother remembers. She conceals the hands beneath the coverlet.

kiss

SHE IS PERFECT, the handsome man says. More perfect than I ever imagined.

He turns to Mother and plunges into a gallant bow: May I?

Mother says, proudly, If you would.

He shoos the brothers and sisters away from the bed and smoothes back his hair, moving with the grace and determination of a maestro. He is nearly overcome with the warmth and fragrance rising from Madeleine's body and pauses, suspended over her, savoring the moment. He imagines how he will describe it, sitting by the hearth, to their flock of children.

He descends for the kiss. It is loud and ardent.

Crouched over, he waits for the blissful response, the two unresisting lips that will succumb and then, hungrily, lunge for more. Crumbs speckle his bristling moustache. Simmering preserves fart in Mother's cauldron. The handsome man waits, stiff as a statue. He discovers that he has developed a cramp in his side.

gift

THE HANDSOME MAN is crestfallen.
  Mother sends him home with a pot of preserves.
  She refuses his money. It's a gift, she insists.

stirring

AS A REWARD for their bravery and cunning, Mother gives the small children delicious bits of the princess's body. They are eaten with enormous appetite.

The brothers and sisters, prickling with crumbs, are allowed to tumble, glutted, into Madeleine's bed. They nuzzle against her and sigh, tucked into the warm pockets of her body. Madeleine stirs in her sleep. She smiles. Mother watches her and wonders, Is she amused by what she dreams?

she dreams

WHEN M. JOUY placed his cock in her palm, it looked accusingly despondent and she was ashamed, for other girls had spoken of its liveliness. But when she wrapped her sturdy fingers around its girth, it shuddered in her grip like an infant bird. She had learned to rattle the orchard trees so that the weakest nestlings would tumble down into the cradle of her hands, where she found pleasure in the jerk and quiver of their frantic breaths. The organ of M. Jouy felt wondrously similar. It struggled against her tightening fingers with soft, bird-like heaves, and she was comforted by knowing that if her attentions grew too avid, its violent heartbeat would not disappear. Too often, a bird's pitiful state would excite in her such an awful tenderness (Oh I love you! I love you! the girl keens to the shivering bird) that she would fondle it to death. Buried in a dung heap, so that the cats cannot sniff out its carious flesh, the bird is wet with tears, its body ravished.

M. Jouy, she said. I have felt this before.

The sad and stately half-wit could not answer, he was so moved by her expertise. She admired how mummy-like he remained while his cock writhed in her hand, as if life had abandoned his body in its eagerness to seek out her touch.

dandelion

SOPHIE HAD INSTRUCTED her to watch his face crumple, majestic
and startling like a damp sheet collapsing from the washline, but
despite the girls' demands—Look, Madeleine, look!—her gaze
never strayed from her hands, his helpless cock.

She wondered at the larger girls who claimed that they were too
old, that the game had become dull. She could never outgrow this;
she would be drawn back ceaselessly, her curiosity constantly
renewed. This she knew: you never tire of decapitating a dandelion
and squeezing out its milky entrails. The more the motion is
repeated, the more irresistible it becomes. You have no choice but
to desecrate a dandelion stalk. That is what it is there for.

His come smelled of the sweet and musty hay that he slept on.
She would kneel down daintily and wipe her hands in the long
grass. As she walked home from the secret place, the village dogs
would nuzzle her palms, their hot tongues lapping up the fading
scent.

pastoral

WHAT HAD SHE DONE differently? She had modeled herself, precisely, on the others: as a very little girl, she stood patiently at the periphery of the ring. As she grew older, she accepted her turn and grabbed hold of M. Jouy without trepidation: she pocketed his pennies, laughed to see his breeches puddled about his ankles, mimicked his lumbering gait. When they dispersed, screeching like crows, she did too. And when they approached the village, suddenly composed and inscrutable, she too fell silent.

We're gathering flowers, she announced, when Mother asked. It made a lovely picture: a procession of girls, filing homeward in the dusk, hands stained green from their efforts. Locals who dreamed of migrating to the city now paused and marveled, What was I thinking? I could not live without these simple pleasures.

curdled milk

WHAT HAD FRIGHTENED the others? Something in the tightness of her grip, or the way her eyes fed upon the cock. She had betrayed no distaste for the game. The other girls crowed to see his defeat, to see his idiot's composure dissolve, and then rushed to wipe themselves clean of his ejaculation. But M. Jouy held no fascination for her; she did not feel triumphant when he brayed and snorted; she was occupied only with the soft, stubborn thing clamped in her fists, and grew reluctant to run her fingers through the long grasses. Every Midsummer morning, Mother woke her before dawn and ordered her to kneel down and bathe her face in the dew: it ensures a year's worth of loveliness, she explained. As a child, Mother had performed the same ritual.

When Madeleine wiped M. Jouy off her hands, she left glistening mollusk trails in the underbrush.

bureaucracy

WHEN AROUSED, even the bucolic village moves with unforgiving swiftness, its machinery oiled and eager. Sophie was eating oatmeal when she decided to tell her mother, and by the time she finished her bowl, her mother had already told her father, who told the priest, who told the mayor. And then it was too late to recant. The mayor puzzled for an afternoon, and by supper had sent his oldest son to fetch the gendarmes. The gendarmes arrived before the sun rose, were directed by a hundred silent fingers towards the barn and apprehended M. Jouy with hay sprouting from his hair, his smile still heavy with dreams.

Madeleine's hands were thrust into a pot of boiling lye.

host

CAN I HAVE SOME MORE? Beatrice asks. She has scrambled down
from the bed and planted herself in Mother's way. I prefer the burnt
part.

Doubling over to stoke the fire, Mother grunts before she gives
her permission. Save some for your father, she says.

Beatrice sidles up to the sleeping princess and surveys the
devastation: one leg lost, from the knee down. The open wound
looks tempting and buttery, but she likes the acrid edges best, where
the dough has blackened, and breaks off an entire hand. Before
biting, she examines it. It looks exactly like the hand of her sleeping
sister: shiny and tempered and mitten-like. The fingers are no
longer articulated because baking has sutured them all into one.

Why did only the hands burn, Maman? she asks through a
mouthful of crumbs.

Because only her hands were wicked, Mother says.

This makes Beatrice pause and consider. Finally, she objects:
She will never be able to sew or play the piano!

It is no great loss. Mother pats her on top of her head, leaving
the floury trace of her five fingertips. And, she adds, they will
always remind her of her childhood. As you grow older, it is often
easy to forget.

Mother hitches her skirts up to her thighs. See. Scars are
remembrances. This slender, sickle-shaped one—she runs her finger
along her shin—reminds me of my best friend, of stealing eggs, of a
shard of glass glinting in the sunshine. And these here—she caresses

the white piping that striates the back of her knees—put me in mind of your grandfather.

Beatrice nods, but secretly she disagrees. When she deposits the last bits into her mouth, she keeps her back turned to Mother. She lowers her eyelids and sticks out her tongue as she has seen the older girls do in church.

she dreams

IN AN OLD HOUSE in Paris that is covered with vines live twelve
little girls in two straight lines.

Madeleine is the twelfth girl. The smallest and the wickedest.
Sister Clavel has been instructed to take special care of her.

How the sisters wept when they first saw her! Her hands
swaddled in snowy strips of muslin, Mother picking absently at the
invisible insects that she feared were infesting the poultices. The
sisters gave Madeleine a brand new prayer book and a straw hat
strangled by a broad brown ribbon. She went with them happily.

The other little girls stroke her bandages as if they were
touching the hem of Christ. Their eyes grow enormous and glassy
and she can hear the prayers escaping beneath their breaths, a slow
hiss of perforated air. At night, as they lie in their two rows, the
moon rises and she shadows it from her cot, her arms arcing like
a ballerina's, her milky fists rising like two false moons, like two
spectral dollops of meringue.

She takes pleasure in her helplessness. Everyone must wait on
her. She cannot even pee by herself. Bernadette, the eleventh girl,
would like eventually to become a saint, so now she is practicing on
Madeleine. She has made it her special duty to clean her when she
menstruates, her little holy hands becoming sticky with the blood.

Bernadette's fingertips are warm when she parts Madeleine's
knees and passes a damp rag between her legs. From her cot,
Madeleine can hear the plash of water against the bowl, the
trickling of fluids as Bernadette wrings the cloth. She waits for the

firm hands that will pat her dry, tuck a clean rag against her wound, press together her splayed thighs. She wonders if the abbot at Rievaulx, when ministering to the bloodied Saint Michel, was as unflinching as Bernadette.

delivery

M. JOUY HAS NOT forgotten Madeleine. On Christmas Day, a
brown paper package arrives from the hospital at Maréville; out of
the package spills a fluttering array of drawings and charts. No
message or holiday wishes enclosed. Mother walks into the village
and asks the local chemist to decipher the contents.

Ahhhh, he murmurs. They have measured M. Jouy's brainpan!
And he holds up the diagram for her to see.

It looks like the moon on its back, Mother observes.

His anatomy is quite regular, no signs of degeneracy, the
chemist continues, peering at a new sheaf. Oh, but look! His
scapula is protuberant.

Shuffling through the papers, the chemist hums to himself, his
spectacles propped on the bald crest of his head. Mother furtively
examines a bottle of whooping cough remedy that within days,
it was rumored, could miraculously resuscitate even the most
exhausted breasts.

So, she interrupts, are they ungodly or not?

Ungodly? the chemist echoes. He frowns briefly. Why, not at all!

Are you sure?

He clutches the drawings: These sketches are the work of
medical professionals! It seems as if M. Jouy would like her to have
them. As a keepsake, perhaps. This picture—he picks out a
physiognomic chart—is a very good likeness.

conversion

THE DRAWINGS ACCUMULATE.

The small brothers and sister discover that they make buoyant kites. Jean-Luc ties one apiece to the posts that support the pasture fence, and on gusty days, the kites swell into the sky, dodging and nodding to one another as if in conversation.

Mother begins to enjoy the delicate swirls of the cranial diagrams, so she cuts them in quarters and decorates her pots of preserves.

custom made

WHEN SISTER CLAVEL lays out her tidy uniform, Madeleine
slips it neatly over her head, and then, with exuberance, her bulky
fists burst through the careful seams, like twin whale snouts
breaking the surface. So it is decided that she must have special
dresses made for her, with long and liquid sleeves like those of an
Oriental concubine. The diminutive tailor clangs the convent bell
and Sister Clavel ushers him up the back stairwell and into a sunlit
room, where Madeleine awaits him, perched on a tiny embroidered
stool, wearing nothing but her stockings. Crouching, the tailor
spreads out his tools, and with an irritating air of indifference, goes
about measuring Madeleine's dimensions. She wonders if she can
be seen from outside. She pictures the next-door neighbor trodding
home, miserable, and then, by chance, he looks up. His smile
spreads: from across the square, the schoolboys let out a blissful,
unanimous sigh in the middle of their verb conjugations. The
nursemaids who perambulate the park peer coyly from beneath
their bonnets, squeezing each other's fingers and giggling naughtily.
And the degenerate man, the one who waits by the rhododendron
bushes, swivels his eyes up to her window, his neck supple as an
owl's, and his cock rises triumphantly out of his breeches.
Meanwhile her bare buttocks warm in a sunbeam and the tailor's
deft fingers slip and alight upon her skin. Madeleine feels, this is
divine.

But when the dresses arrive, cocooned in crisp tissue paper, they are not the gossamer confections that she has imagined; indeed, they make her appear even more uncanny: half-child, half-beast. The bodice and skirt are indistinguishable from the convent uniform, austere and shapeless and busy with buttons, but the arms: they droop like two flaccid elephant ears.

scherzo

PERHAPS IT IS THOSE unwieldy arms that make the gypsies love
her so. They pluck her from the crowd as if she were the roundest
and ripest fruit, and the eleven other girls squirm with envy. A
disappearing trick! Sister Clavel wrings her hands; outings make her
perspire and she is happy only when her charges are praying or
asleep. Madeleine smiles at them from the center of the ring as the
gypsy mama unspools, from one of her several and cavernous
pockets, an endless piece of string.

Displaying it for all the crowd to see, she secures the greasy end
between Madeleine's fists and circles around her with the swiftness
of a spider until Madeleine looks like a well-wrapped fly. Can she
breathe? Sister Clavel worries, while Bernadette steels herself,
preparing to make the rescue.

The little package is raised aloft by the gypsy mama, and then
tossed, with a series of shouts, from one epicene acrobat to another.
Firecrackers hiss and the sickly, frail animals begin to fret inside
their cages. The audience stomp their feet like tribesmen, join in
the chanting of the gypsy words, and suddenly, from out of the
cacophony, there rises a wounded wail; the midgets scurry, brushing
aside a velvet curtain, behind which sits a beautiful woman, who
saws upon her own tautly stretched hairs with the energy of the
devil. Her costly dress gapes open, her fingers jig up and down her
elegant neck, and her bow bobs back and forth across her belly. The
faster she plays, the more her face glows: she is self-illuminating,
ecstatic, and her strange, discolored song makes the gypsies dance

with the desperation of a bear on a chain. They gravitate towards her, yelping, and Madeleine comes flying with them, shuttling over their heads as they reel in tightening circles around the stringed beauty, whose bow moves so quickly it blurs. She scrapes harder, faster, more frantically, her knees atremble, and then: the bow clatters to the ground, the strings jangle, and the player gasps. The spell is cast.

Cuddling it in her arms, the gypsy mama returns the ball of string to center stage. A hush falls over the tent. Is the little girl propped on her head or on her feet? By now it is impossible to tell. Shhhhhhhhhhhh! the mama commands. See and be amazed!

After a peremptory wiggle of her fingers, she grabs the frayed end of string and yanks it.

evanescent

OFF THE BUNDLE GOES, spinning like a top. It leaves a trail of string in its wake, tracing a desultory pattern across the floor. When it skitters out to the edges of the ring, Bernadette swoops down and opens her arms, but as soon as she can feel its whir, away it goes in the opposite direction, obeying a gravity of its own. Its progress is dizzying; heaps of string litter the stage. The bulge unravels into a ghost of its former self, until all that is left is a latticework of twine, suspended, still quivering, in midair.

Madeleine has vanished.

visitor

MOTHER IS STARTLED by a thunderous thump, and Madeleine moans in her sleep. Looking up from her cauldron, she sees Papa, cheek flattened against the warm flank of a cow, arm extended and pointing placidly at their roof. Matilde has alighted there, and left droppings beside their chimney.

Mother bustles outside and gestures at Matilde with her spoon: Not today, Madame, please! Madeleine is sleeping.

The wings of the fat woman swell: I am conducting a scientific experiment. I should not be long.

She stoops down and sniffs her droppings. Roses! she announces. It smells like roses!

How wicked! Mother gasps and seeks shelter inside, her head protruding from the door so that she can remind Matilde: Only the saints' bones should smell like roses. You must have made a mistake.

impostor

MADELEINE IS AWOKEN by the reek of roses, and when she opens
her eyes, she sees the gypsy mama, swabbing off her dusky
complexion with a handkerchief soaked in rosewater. Beneath,
her skin is tuber pale and porous.

So you are not a real gypsy? Madeleine asks, extracting herself
from the depths of a flabby divan.

Heavens no! the woman exclaims. I was only acting.

Then please take me back to Sister Clavel, Madeleine says with
decision.

The woman laughs, and her voice pirouettes in the air like one
of her willowy acrobats: You may call me Marguerite, she says.

And then she resumes at the mirror.

alchemy

IT IS NO MISTAKE. Matilde has made a survey of her own droppings, keeping assiduous record of her mood, the direction of the wind, the sun's position in the sky. Since she has taken flight, she is most often seen scratching away in the leatherbound diary she keeps stashed between her breasts: leaning up against someone's chimney, or resting in the crotch of a pear tree, her stubby legs dangling cheerfully. In the left-hand column, the data: a loaf of bread and half a pot of preserves; buttermilk; leg of lamb with mint sauce; beer; feeling melancholy; a moderate breeze from the southeast; sun barely past the church spire. In the right-hand column, the results, which are inexorably the same: chalky color, pasty to the touch, and redolent with roses.

The scientific spirit has infected Matilde; like her, these droppings are the product of inexplicable change. Atop the village's roofs, which now serve as her laboratory, she hitches up her skirts and relieves herself. She contemplates the evidence and is puzzled by the enormity of the transformation—the seedy strawberries, the marbled side of ham, the bumpy rind on a wheel of Camembert— all reduced, distilled, made uniform: nothing is left of them except this puddle of excrement, white as an eggshell, and fragrant as June.

Jean-Luc, who has been waiting for her visit, climbs over Claude and slides out of the bed. Before Mother can catch him, he has rushed out of the house and hoisted himself onto the trellis. He trembles on the highest rung, but only his forehead rises over the edge of the thatching.

Pardon me! he cries.

Matilde leans over the edge to see him better. Her bulk casts a shadow over Jean-Luc's upturned face.

My kites got tangled, he says, and jerks his head towards the pasture, where a fragile forest of kites has knotted itself into a skein. They flap fretfully against the sky.

Will you please untangle them? he asks.

Matilde squints at him. She recognizes his froggy voice, remembers that he could throw far and accurately. She suddenly misses her slow and suety processions. Astride a rooftop, above the hubbub of those bound by gravity, she longs for the market days when she paraded down the street.

Very well, she agrees and struggles to her feet, her wings thrashing the air. Jean-Luc loses his balance and tumbles down into Mother's gesticulating arms.

stripped

THE GYPSY CAMP is disappointing in its tidiness. No smoking fires, no wagons painted in raffish reds and golds, no unmentionables hanging from the windows to dry. Instead, the camp is an outpost of sorts, a miniature rococo fantasy: the creamy-colored caravans are ornamented with flutings and fig leafs, and brocade curtains hunker in the doorways. In the gypsy mama's window boxes, a tiny but well-manicured topiary grows where geraniums ought to be straggling.

Madeleine's bandaged hands have wilted by her sides, and she slumps dejectedly on her stool. Trying to cheer her, Marguerite waves a pair of glittering shears in the air, as long and keen as a sword.

Be brave, she instructs Madeleine. Don't move a muscle.

The scissors dive down between Madeleine's shallow breasts, she shivers, and Marguerite brings the blades together with a snap. The monstrous dress falls to her feet, neatly cleft in two.

A sartorial disaster, Marguerite says as she repockets her enormous shears. She settles down onto her haunches: Now, give me one of your hands.

And she takes hold of the little bundle, so dear that she can hardly bear to touch it, like a butterfly collector cradling a cocoon. Her fingers fly over the bandages as if they were reading Braille; soon she has discovered and disinterred the ragged end.

Madeleine watches mildly as the punished hand is unwrapped.

She sees that her hand has healed.

The fingers have mended together, sewn up tightly along the seams.

My hand looks like a paddle, Madeleine says.

That might prove useful, Marguerite replies.

la lucrezia

MADELEINE STARES DOWN at the two paddles sitting in her lap.

An accident? Marguerite inquires.

Madeleine shakes her head.

I feared not, the woman sighs.

And straightening up, she resumes a conversation that Madeleine can't recall their ever having:

Among the first parts written for me was Lucretia. An old story: a woman raped by the son of a tyrannical king. There is nothing left of her but shame and rage. From hell I shall seek his ruin, she sings. With savage and implacable fury. And then she does herself in at the end. Sword through the breast—I pantomimed the whole thing. The Marquis Ruspoli said he felt shivers running up and down his spine.

When the composer came to kiss my hand, I hissed at him, Don't ever write such a role for me again.

Marguerite draws her scissors from her pocket as though she were unsheathing a terrible blade.

I told him, Make me a general. Make me a son. If you give me a sword, let me bury it in Ptolemy's side. For who wants to be a woman wronged? With no recourse but wretchedness and death?

Not I, Marguerite declares, her blade flashing. Not I!

Her gaze falls suddenly upon Madeleine, who is caught unawares. She thought that Marguerite, in the throes of her story, had forgotten her.

The woman narrows her eyes: Do you understand me?

The girl shrugs. I suppose so.

Marguerite takes the injured hands in her own and says, coldly, You are disgraced. Disfigured. So what will you do now?

Madeleine announces an idea that has occurred to her only a few seconds before, as she reflected on how pleasant it felt to be wearing only her underclothes. She says, with dignity: I plan on being a tumbler. Or a contortionist. Whichever I am better at.

Marguerite claps her hands. Her severity gives way, in an instant, to laughter.

My dear child! she cries, voice lifting into song.

If drinking is bitter, Marguerite sings, become wine.

palimpsest

THE SMALL BROTHERS and sisters receive a letter from Madeleine! The envelope is bedecked with bright, mysterious stamps. After gingerly prying open the seal, Beatrice smoothes the contents against her chest, delighting in the crackling fragility of the paper, and then lifts it above her head as the others clamber about her. Mother quiets them in the folds of her skirts so that Beatrice can read the letter aloud:

She is happy at the convent, she says. The other girls like her very much and she has a bed of her own to sleep in. Bernadette is the name of the girl who is kind enough to write this letter for her (Beatrice exclaims over the loveliness of her handwriting). She gives each one of us a kiss (Beatrice delivers kisses) and she prays for us every night before she goes to sleep. Love, Madeleine.

Very good, Mother says, and heads out to the shed to tell Papa that everything has turned out as it should.

Once alone, the children huddle together while Beatrice brings down a candle from the mantelpiece. The wick flares, and they are breathless in their conspiracy. Madeleine has taught them the secret language of siblings, the head flicks and eye rolls and coded words, and now, true enough, she has buried another letter beneath the surface of the first, a letter meant especially for them. Beatrice holds the parchment up to the flame and the effaced writing becomes translucently visible. Written in lemon juice, of course! She sighs at her sister's cleverness. So she tells aloud the second story, the one inscribed in invisible ink, and the children sit around her, rapt.

I do not miss anyone at all, she says. I live with gypsies. I have learned to stretch my feet back behind my head and waddle about on my hands. Yesterday a photographer appeared and asked to take our portraits. He stood me between the dog girl and the flatulent man and told me to display my hands as if they were the crown jewels. What a fool, his buttocks sticking out from behind his machinery. In the picture, we will all be laughing.

scriptor

CHARLOTTE PAUSES in mid-flourish. Are you going to tell them about me?

New paragraph: I know a woman who looks like a viol, Madeleine dictates.

method

BOXING JEAN-LUC'S EARS, Mother is struck by an idea. She hurries off towards the pasture, where Matilde is wrestling with kites.

Madame! Mother hollers up to the sky. Please share some tarte aux pommes with me.

Matilde disentangles herself: Happily!

She sails down from the heights like a mighty barge, then politely collapses her wings and strolls alongside Mother.

The two take their tea outside, on a stone bench warm from the afternoon sun. Matilde asks after the children.

I am so busy now, Mother sighs. My children are growing wild like weeds. I can't read them as well as I used to: Jean-Luc crept out from right under my nose! In earlier days, I would have known his wicked thoughts before even he did, and been waiting for him, arms outstretched, when he slid out from beneath the covers. Please forgive him for interrupting your experiments!

Matilde tsks: I wasn't bothered. She pats Mother's hand.

You are a woman of science, Mother ventures.

Matilde nods.

Then perhaps you can help me! Mother says.

Matilde gestures for her to continue.

When Madeleine sleeps, Mother explains, she smiles. Sometimes she sighs. Sometimes she is as still as a log. But these signs are so small and faint, as if coming from a great distance, and I cannot decipher them.

Matilde extracts her leatherbound diary from deep within her cleavage. As she opens the book, its pages fan out like a peacock's tail. I have filled a volume, she says, describing small and mysterious signs. I have yet to see the pattern, but I know that it will emerge.

She presses Mother's hands against the pages: One day I will be leafing through my book, and suddenly the signs will become sensible. They will reveal themselves as a language, a story. That is what I am waiting for.

She lifts Mother's hands from the pages. Shutting the diary, Matilde tucks it back between her breasts.

le petomane

THE MOUTH OF the ink bottle still gleams wetly, but once the moaning begins, Charlotte shudders and finds that she can write no further.

Poor M. Pujol, she sighs.

Madeleine nods solemnly. The flatulent man, pale and elegant and tall, suffers from bad dreams, owing to the sordid company he kept during his reign in Paris.

A modest and elegant man, he never speaks of his former brilliance, but once, when Madeleine was practicing her contortions, he gently unfolded her and grasped her paddle in one of his warm hands. Behind the nearest caravan, he bowed slightly, lifted the tails of his well-cut coat and produced the most melancholy sounds she had ever heard: that of the nightingale, the grasshopper, the cuckoo. And though Madeleine was a child who rarely cried, the strange and unearthly emissions reminded her of her home, and she wept.

Charlotte, too, is crying. She hears in the nightmare moans of M. Pujol a voice that she misses.

performance

M. PUJOL FINDS IT strangely fitting that his performance should now excite tears, when once he could reduce an entire theatre to gasping and painful hilarity. How could such a simple and surely familiar act produce such paroxysms of laughter? On stage: a sad, pale-faced man; a large basin of water; a candlestick sitting atop a stool. In the seats: gentlemen and their wives, their mouths flung wide open, their hands clawing at the velveteen armrests. M. Pujol believes that his art is akin to that of the oboist, or the bassoonist: a matter of shaping the lips around a stream of air. The fact that his lips should belong to his lower regions, that his should be endowed with unusual agility and musicality, does not strike him as remarkable. But the pleasure that his gift brings to others! Due to the tightness of their corsets, and the violence of their laughter, women often lose consciousness altogether. They are carried out by swarthy nurses, whom the manager Oller has stationed in the aisles—cunningly—for this very purpose.

The little boy who sweeps the floor finds it strewn with discarded collars, shredded handkerchiefs, pearly buttons trailing bits of thread. It is a phenomenon that M. Pujol has witnessed from the stage: this peculiar compulsion to disrobe, to rend from the body its restraints. He lifts his tailcoat, he farts; the whole house convulses. Le Petomane watches, aghast, as below him bodies burst forth from their envelopes. The audience stretches before him, a field in late summer, crackling pods splitting at their seams, releasing into the air armies of weightless and dancing spores.

invasion

THE GIFT REVEALED ITSELF to him when he was only a child, and visiting the seashore with his family. His younger sister had been possessed by a growling cough all winter; it was thought that the air might restore her. Joseph, as he was then called, was the first to venture into the water. The sea licked at him like an icy tongue; his skin prickled; his genitals retreated. But inside he felt the warm thrumming of his own small body, the quiet roar of his blood, as if he had swallowed a wonderful little engine that kicked up its own heat. I am still warm in here! he rejoiced silently.

Joseph! his mother cried. He saw her, beautiful and slim, silhouetted by the bathing hut. Joseph! she cried. Do not swallow the seawater! It will burn your nostrils terribly! It will go right up into your brain!

He pinched the tip of his nose firmly between his fingers. He expanded his lungs, he puffed out his cheeks. He counted to seven. Then the water closed over him, sealing him inside its cold and salty mouth. The little engine panted away, and Joseph could hear the quickening thumps as the men, caps pushed back and sweating, heaved more coal into its radiant belly. I'm warm! Joseph crowed. It's working! He held the sea at bay; he curled up beside the hot, vibrating machine.

And then the unthinkable occurred. A gasket burst, perhaps, or a valve failed. The unreliable sphincter! Joseph felt the icy water enter him, felt it storming down his narrow corridors, felt it surging into the hold. The chamber flooded; the engine's glowing belly was extinguished; the engineers' caps bobbed sadly atop the cold and salty sea that had invaded him. His abdomen contracted in a series of agonizing and colicky spasms.

On shore, behind an outcropping of white stones, squatting above the sand, he expelled a stomach's worth of sea. It bubbled briefly, then disappeared.

diagnosis

INSIDE THE BATHING HUT, the wide-striped curtains flapping wildly, Joseph confessed to his beautiful mother: I think I've got a very bad illness.

How terrible! she said, and gathered him to her, where he squeezed his eyes shut, listened to the thud of the canvas slapping against the poles, smelled the unfamiliar newness of her bathing costume, and tried to ignore the intractable cold that had settled deep inside him. There is a doctor staying at the hotel, his mother said. We will call on him this afternoon.

The doctor was delighted by the boy's condition. He pointed to the chamberpot, sitting in the middle of an expensive Persian carpet, and demanded, Do it again!

Joseph obliged. He allowed the water to enter him, and then he asked it back out again. As it gurgled into the basin, the doctor clapped his hands together in astonishment. Quite fantastic! he cried. His muscular control is extraordinary!

Joseph's mother accepted the compliment with evident pleasure. But she wanted to be certain: It is not an illness?

Far from it, he assured. An abnormality, certainly, but I consider it, as should you, an endowment!

With a waving of his hands, the doctor indicated that the examination was now over, and that Joseph could pull up his shorts and resume a more dignified position.

The muscles can be strengthened, the doctor said, but that will require careful training. Imagine a trajectory of at least several meters, like those of the magnificent fountains at Versailles. And if he can inhale water in such a manner, it stands to reason he can do the same with other substances. He can take in air, like a bellows, and learn to release it with direction and force. Can't you see it: the boy who blows out candles with his backside. The boy with the breathing bunghole!

The doctor sighed rapturously. He did not, in fact, belong to the medical profession. He had assumed the title of doctor as a reflection of his expertise in all matters hypnotic, clairvoyant, and supernatural. He had studied and improved upon the writings of Dr. Mesmer; he had enjoyed considerable success on both the spiritualist and vaudevillian circuits. The doctor believed that no one was better suited than he to recognize a great talent and, moreover, he was acquainted with an impresario who would see the possibilities of the enterprise. How fortunate, he thought, that this dear woman and her extraordinary child should have come to me, rather than a medical practitioner. Joseph and his mother, of course, were unaware of their mistake, for the doctor, not being a man of rigid principles, neglected to alert them. He wore a William II moustache that Joseph admired, and would one day emulate, when he was a grown man.

lesson

CHARLOTTE, her face still gleaming wetly, unbuttons the bodice of
her dress, draws her bow across the strings. She will accompany the
nocturnal torments of M. Pujol, in the hope that he will cease his
moaning. The sleeping man's anguish, released into the night, has
now become her own: with each cry, M. Pujol conjures her former
face and companion, Griselda.

Listen, Madeleine.

The viol sighs. The girl sits beside her.

You should listen. Music, more than any other thing in the
world, teaches us emotion.

The viol grows agitated.

Pathos! Fury!

The viol sobs.

Longing. Desire.

Madeleine tells herself to listen hard, for she wants to expand
her meager vocabulary. She has taken inventory and discovered the
emptiness of her shelves: Curiosity; Amusement; Grumpiness;
Delight; Disappointment. That is the extent of it.

Spreading herself onto the caravan's floor, she presses her cheek
against the floorboards, her paddles resting like two loyal dogs on
either side of her face. She instructs her ear to pay strict attention.
But as Charlotte sways beside her, the bow seesawing furiously,
Madeleine finds that it is not her ear but her very body that is being
exercised. The song rises up through her limbs, her heart, her
stomach, like heat from a flat and sun-soaked rock, and deep within

her something begins to reverberate, as if her own hidden strings have been set aquiver. There is only one emotion she feels, not the spectacular and edifying range that Charlotte has promised: no fury, no pathos, no longing. Just a wild tumult inside her.

Charlotte, she says from the floor. I could do that!

She points at the strings, the flickering bow: When you play, I feel as if I could play, too. As if to play so beautifully were as easy as taking and releasing a breath. As easy as falling asleep and having a dream.

stirring

MADELEINE STIRS in her sleep.

indolent

AS FAR AS MOTHER UNDERSTANDS, hers is not the only family
ever to experience calamity. Daughters wander off into the woods,
stumble into prostitution, fall in love with sailors, are eaten by
wolves. When Mother was a child, she knew of a shapely girl who
was plucked from her bath by a large and lice-ridden bird; it held
her dripping from its talons and then, squawking merrily, took to
the sky. The girl's family left the tub out by the barn, in the hope
that once the bird tired of her company, it might return her to her
bath. Over time the tub rusted and rattled; sometimes mice would
scamper over its edge and drown.

But the misfortunes of other families seem always to involve
disappearance or abduction. The girl is missed; she is mourned; she
is remembered as bonny and helpful and light on her feet. What
a loss! What a shame! Women clasp their daughters to their breasts
and whisper horrors into their ears: Darkness. Appetites. Trees. And
no moon to light your way.

And then there is Madeleine, who doesn't seem to be going
anywhere; who takes up room; who attracts attention; who lies
there, sighing voluptuously, as Mother sweats over the fire.

Nothing makes one's own work more difficult than being in
the presence of another's idleness. The sight of Madeleine, stretched
upon the bed, begins to try her mother's patience. Occasionally,
she grows careless with the handle of her broom. Accidentally, she
sets the pots aclattering. In the middle of the night, she undertakes
an experiment: when a candle drips its wax onto Madeleine's cheek,
it sets into motion a most fascinating series of twitches.

she dreams

GYPSIES, IT SEEMS, can no longer captivate a crowd. A woman who looks like a viol, a girl who waddles on the seared stumps of her hands, a man who sings from his backside, are incapable of provoking wonder. The procession of gypsy caravans trundles from one empty venue to the next. The fearsome Marguerite, who once wore a sword, who once played the hero, finds herself dangerously close to despair.

Miraculously, a summons arrives. The photographer has circulated his portraits among the wealthy of Toulouse. A widow, renowned for her fecund imagination, purchases every last photograph and hangs them all in her high-ceilinged drawing room. She sits, daily, for several hours, in this gallery of grotesques. One Sunday, when the lilacs are in bloom, she becomes animated by an idea. She wishes the company to pay her a visit, at her expense. She has a proposition.

depraved

LIKE THIS? Madeleine asks, paddle suspended in midair.

Just so, the widow says.

The girl's hand falls squarely upon the backside of M. Pujol. *Smack!* is the sound of her palm meeting the flesh of his bared cheeks. His elegant tailcoat, his white butterfly tie, his black satin breeches, are folded neatly in a pile that sits by the door.

Louder, the widow says, from her chair. She cups a hand around her ear.

indivisible

THE GYPSIES install themselves on the velvety lawns that surround the house. From a window, high above them, the widow watches as the performers step out from their caravans. Here they are, in the sunlight, on the grass; there they were, in the candlelight, on the carpet. The sight wounds her, fills her with pleasure: yes, those are the same bodies, the same gentle souls. How could that be? How could the child tumbling along the shrubbery be the child who wielded her misshapen hands with such stimulating results? How could the man brushing out his coat be the man who flinched, and shivered, and moaned? And she, is she the same, standing with a Sèvres cup, looking out the window of her house?

As a very small child, she was told the story of a tailor who, for fear of losing his shadow, secured it to himself with stitches. This is how she imagines it: a woman sitting in a chair, in the candlelight, cupping her ear, is stitched onto the woman standing here with a Sèvres cup in her hand. And she knows that, as with all things sutured, the two leaves cannot be separated without destroying them both. She is certain of it. Yet she persists in picking at the edges; she delights in seeing how the wound seeps, where the scab has been lifted away by a fingernail.

talent

EVERYONE'S TALENT is put to use. Madeleine paddles. M. Pujol moans. Charlotte plays. The photographer composes. He, too, has succumbed to the widow's proposition. His name is Adrien, and he is the younger brother of a famous and sought-after man who practices the same trade as he, except with greater success. That celebrated photographer counts among his sitters Victor Hugo, Gustave Flaubert, the divine Sarah Bernhardt.

It is thanks to him that Adrien now finds his second-rate skills in demand. As assistant to his more capable brother, he has toured the catacombs and sewers of Paris, taking pictures underground, learning to illuminate dark places. Places no darker than the widow's drawing room at night.

Adrien shyly takes hold of Madeleine and turns her face to the light. She rustles when he moves her, layer upon layer of starched petticoat, shiny frock, drooping bow, rising up around her like froth on boiling milk. She submits to his touch with a tender complaisance, as if she likes nothing better than being arranged. But now he must fix the sad and pale-faced man. Try as he might, the photographer cannot make him understand. He must arch his back so; he must let his head drop between his arms; he must appear more dog-like. It is as the widow wishes. In exasperation, Adrien presses his hand into the small of M. Pujol's back: Like so!

He withdraws his hand, in fear. The shock of this man's skin against his fingertips: it is something he has not felt before. Through the camera's round eye, the man is bright as a planet, his naked body whiter and more brilliant than the explosion that, for a single hot second, illuminates the room.

swan

IF THIS WERE A MYTH, then Madeleine would be the swan: wings beating, fingers webbed, with all the powers of a god.

And M. Pujol? He is overtaken; he is hot with shame.

abasement

IN THE STARLIGHT, behind the shrubbery, M. Pujol practices his scales. Although his backside has now been put to other uses, and the only sounds he utters are those involuntary moans, he dreams of one day returning to the stage. What a pity that the widow expresses no interest in his true talent. If only she could hear his repertoire: this the timid fart of the young girl, this the bride on her wedding night (very little) and the morning after (very loud), this the dressmaker tearing two yards of calico, this the storm clouds thundering in the sky, this the cannon defending the coastline. Surely, it would delight her. Surely, she could sponsor his triumphant return!

He confides to Madeleine: I think if I were to do one or two vocalizations. . . .

But it is hopeless. The widow is a woman of voluptuous tastes and wide experience; only the prudish could take pleasure in his gift. The body's eruptions, he realizes, hold no power over those who have moved beyond embarrassment. How terrible it is to recognize that one's brilliance rests solely upon the small-mindedness of others.

M. Pujol's head droops from his long and elegant neck.

The widow has selected him, it seems, for no reason other than his William II moustache, his Ledaen body. His expression of sweet, dreaming melancholy.

touch

THE BURN OF the chestnut too hot from the fire? The sting of a wasp in late summer? The prick of a burr, stuck in your side, as you crash through the brambles?

Adrien peers at his inflamed fingertips.

No, that's not it. That's not it at all.

rectitude

AFTER THE LAST CANDLE has been extinguished, and the widow
has withdrawn to her chambers, the performers gather on the
lawn, where they listen to the flatulent man tell stories of celebrity
and betrayal. M. Pujol, once so reluctant to speak of his past, has
been changed by his rather precipitous decline. He is now possessed
by the need to recount his days in Paris; he must make his
companions understand that his life has not been one spent upon
the hands and knees.

He is most emphatic on this particular point. I was a man of
great stature, he says, flinging his arms high above his head. I always
performed upright!

I had a pretty little English carriage, a cabriolet drawn by a mare
named Aida, and when I drove it through town, dressed in my very
best, I was recognized and saluted wherever I went. People loved to
joke, Is that Le Petomane who just passed?

With my name at the top of the bill, the theatre prospered, the
owner and the manager growing fat off the ticket sales and lavishing
praise on me, who had brought them such good fortune. They
hosted extravagant parties after my performances, their stiff
shirtfronts turning scarlet with spilt wine, pomegranate seeds, the
dribblings of fuddled dancing girls. What a *wind*-fall! they would
toast, their shouts of laughter hurting my ears and making me
tremble with disgust.

So I would beg indigestion, and the manager would shuffle

me out. Aida would then take me home, her hooves clocking along the empty streets, and I would try to improve my spirits by recalling the precise moment when the audience burst open before me.

I am Le Petomane! I would tell myself. I am a source of astonishment and delight!

impostor

UNTIL THE ARRIVAL of an impostor, M. Pujol sighs. Marguerite looks up sharply from Madeleine's hands, which she is dressing with a balm made of beeswax and camomile.

I'm quite sure that Oller, wily man that he was, recruited her from the brothel he frequented. She called herself La Femme-Petomane and, of course, she was entirely fraudulent. Oh, the trickery made possible by a woman's attire! A woman, after she has completed her toilet, is like a house of illusions: a thick waist is turned slender, a shallow bosom appears ample, nothing is as it appears! The false petomane was no different. Within the dark recesses of her skirts, she hid a wind-making device, perhaps as simple as the bellows one finds beside the fireplace.

Because her emissions were of an artificial nature, they necessarily lacked the musicality and nuance of my own, but this is a distinction that the public failed to make. How they loved her! How they laughed at her crudities! You must remember that I always conducted myself with the utmost dignity and restraint. This she dispatched with immediately, and the audience seemed not to miss it, but instead roared all the harder at seeing a woman perform the feats that I had invented and perfected. The very fact of her femininity seemed only to heighten their shock and their pleasure.

A broken man, I was taken in by our kind benefactress, and thus I find myself a member of this charming company.

blush

M. PUJOL OFFERS Marguerite a bow, which she accepts with a shrug of her shoulders.

Yes, we are all tricks and illusions, she wryly observes. As opposed to you, who are naked, and utterly without artifice.

The flatulent man blushes.

burn

AND SO DOES MADELEINE. And to flush this way, for his sake—as though a blush were contagious, as though it could spread like Roman fever through the night air—it alarms her. She does not understand what is happening. She wrestles her hands away from Marguerite, then flees, racing across the black lawns, seeking water: a fountain, a fish pond, troughs in the stables, the pump outside the kitchen door—just water, please. Away she runs, made swift by terror, looking for a cool, dark place; for wetness; relief.

She has felt this once before: this slow, corrosive burn.

in the orangerie

M. PUJOL TOSSES an orange high into the air. He believes he is alone; he hums a tune; he tosses the orange higher and higher, so that when it grazes the foot of a dryad frisking on the ceiling, and a little bit of painted plaster comes tumbling down from above, M. Pujol freezes, and then, with the toe of his elegant shoe, guides the bit of plaster behind a column. He drops the orange.

Are you going to eat that? Madeleine asks. She is standing outside in the sunlight, a small fierce shadow looking in.

Oh yes! The flatulent man stoops to retrieve it.

What a pleasure it is, he says, to eat an orange in the afternoon.

Seating himself on a wrought iron chair, he presses his thumbnail into the rind. Madeleine continues to stare at him, hungry and implacable.

Forgive me, M. Pujol cries in embarrassment. We will both have oranges!

And moving through the trees, he cups oranges in his hands, brings them up to his nose. After sniffing, he decides; he grasps and pulls; the little tree bends forward and then snaps back, shivering.

Catch! he says, throwing the orange at the girl, the orange arcing like a sun, the girl catching it in the great dull mitts of her hands.

He resumes peeling.

She looks down at her hands, at the intractable orange.

His long fingers ease the rind from the flesh, sending up a mist, a sigh, a tearing sound. As M. Pujol peels, he releases into the air the scent of oranges. He is absorbed in keeping the rind whole, a rough skin unfurling from his fingers.

He glances up at Madeleine. She is still standing there, mute, studying her orange.

Oh! His embarrassment is complete.

Would you allow me? he asks, starting from his chair, reaching out to the girl, spilling his orange from his lap, and watching it bounce across the floor. M. Pujol falters, unsure of whether to rescue Madeleine from her predicament, or the orange from the floor, which he then might offer to her in apology. But the orange will be dirtied and bruised; the girl will be made more unhappy; the orange has rolled its way to the feet of the girl. He must pick it up, must make amends, and so he stands and bends at the waist, attempting in his confusion to both bow to the girl and recover the orange, and as he does so, as he is bending over, she sees the soft hair growing along the back of his neck, just as it would on the neck of a boy, and she is surprised.

petted

SHE WOULD LIKE to touch the soft hair growing there on the back of his neck: it is the palest, finest pelt, like that of a very young child. She would like to stretch out a finger and stroke it, so tenderly that even he would not know that he had been touched. But she cannot brush against anything with just a fingertip. Were she to touch M. Pujol, he would feel a paw. He would feel a warm weight falling eagerly, clumsily, on the back of his neck.

The flatulent man straightens; the silvery pelt vanishes beneath his collar; he is holding out his hand to take her orange. May I, he asks, and when she relinquishes it, she finds that all the pleasure she once took in her disfigurement—the pleasure of being waited upon, petted, made a spectacle of—all that pleasure has disappeared.

inept

TO EVERYONE'S SURPRISE, the photographer, whose fingers are nimble, whose tread is light, whose every movement is small and inconspicuous, has become suddenly, wretchedly, clumsy. Glass plates slip from his grasp and shatter into fragments on the floor. He trips over carpets, over doorstops; he trips as he is walking down the widow's marble hallways. From his darkroom come cries of misery and exasperation. The performers become impatient; many photographs must be retaken. Their necks grow stiff from holding the same stultifying pose.

It is M. Pujol, however, who suffers most. The photographer is forever bumping into him. When he stumbles, it is always in M. Pujol's direction that he falls. The photographer cannot, it seems, refill his wine glass, wash his hands, extract his handkerchief, illustrate a point, without somehow getting in M. Pujol's way. Their soapy knuckles knock against each other in the basin. They reach for the bottle at the same time, and their forearms brush. During the course of a lively conversation, it often happens that the back of Adrien's gesticulating hand will hit M. Pujol in the face.

The flatulent man finds himself apologizing even more often than he usually does. But the photographer is ungracious; though he is the one who always bumps and crowds, he never asks for forgiveness. He never once says, Pardon me. Instead, he skulks behind a caravan, where he furtively examines his knuckles, his arm, the back of his hand, as if it were he who stood the greatest risk of being bruised.

in the candlelight

LOUDER, THE WIDOW SAYS, leaning forward in her chair.

by the folly

M. PUJOL IS CHARMED by his reflection: he appears enormous! There he is, in the still waters of the fishpond, looking nearly as tall as the temple that rises up behind him. He sits down upon its crumbling steps. Of course, he has not really grown; it is only that the temple is perfectly small.

There was once a widow, M. Pujol says, to no one in particular. He is alone.

And it seems that he has gone mad, that failure and humiliation have destroyed his sense, but indeed he has not, or at least not yet, for this afternoon he has an audience, whom he spotted in the mirror of the fishpond. A small figure, unannounced, crouching in the reeds, watching him. She has taken off her stockings and her boots. The hem of her white dress drifts in the water.

And the widow, M. Pujol continues, loved all beautiful things. But she was very old, and decrepit, and had barely the strength to leave her rooms. She said to her gardener, Dig me a pond; I will sit by my window and the sight of it will soothe me. Then she said: Fill my pond with fish, so that I might see their scales flashing in the sunlight.

A voice from the reeds says: I know a widow.

The gardener did as she wished, but one by one the fish began to disappear. The gardener told the widow, There is an orange carp that is slowly devouring the contents of your pond. Unless I kill him, he will eat all the other fish, and you will no longer be able to look at them. But the widow said: He is the most beautiful; he is my favorite. Let him do as he likes.

A voice from the reeds says: She lives in a very grand house.

So the carp grew to a gigantic size. He spent his days turning lazily about the pond, the sun glinting off his prodigious scales. Reflections swayed across the ceiling of the widow's room, so that now, even from her bed, she could take pleasure in her carp. All summer long he illuminated her ceiling, and when she wheeled herself to the window and peered down into her pond, he seemed to grow even more languorous, even more indifferent, as though he could feel her watching him.

justice

BUT THEN a thunderstorm descended, and a lightning bolt struck the widow's pond.

Laughter erupts from the reeds. The audience's sense of justice is delighted.

bloodless

YES; ONE WOULD THINK the carp had died. The gardener was
certain of it: he brought with him a net to drag the fish out from
the water. As he neared the pond, he spied a pale shape slipping
beneath the surface—not a shape but a shade, belonging perhaps
to a ghostly carp. Upon closer inspection, however, the gardener
found the fish very much alive; the accident had simply drained
him of color.

After his encounter with the lightning bolt, the carp resumed
his lazy circles about the pond. Instead of resembling a great golden
shield, flashing in the green depths of the water, the fish was now
mistaken, by turns, for a sunken chamberpot, an abandoned
bedsheet, for the swollen arm of a drowned woman.

moral

FROM THE REEDS, a voice says: And so the gardener killed the carp. The widow wished him to.

M. Pujol asks, How did you know?

A stone is sent splashing into the water. Madeleine says, This pond doesn't have any fish.

For the first time, M. Pujol notices this. No, he says, it doesn't.

Who is the carp? Madeleine asks.

Oh, M. Pujol says. No one. That story is only to say, I'm afraid of the widow.

nothing

THE GIRLS OF THE VILLAGE have all disappeared. Who will bring in the goats? Who will set the table? Mothers stand in doorways, looking provoked. Their daughters are nowhere to be found, although the twilight is filled with names: Marianne! Sophie! Emma! Beatrice!

Those girls. Wedded to mischief. What will we do with them?

A cry rises up from the far field: Aha!

Papa has discovered them.

And he will bellow; he will make them hurry home. The tall grasses parting, their caps gone askew, they'll come spilling out, red-faced, mock-penitent, grinning with secrets.

But all is quiet. Papa has not made a sound.

He is too surprised to speak. Aha! he had shouted, and at once the girls stiffened—hands outstretched, knees deep in the grass. Now Beatrice sits upright, blinking wildly, petals shedding from her face, her breasts, the dark fall of her hair. She has been laid out on the grass; she has been strewn with flowers. The girls have been tending to her: they touched her skin, and spread her hair; they held a mirror beneath her nose.

Before Papa has even the breath to ask, the girls answer his question:

Nothing, they murmur. It's nothing

game

BEATRICE IS ENRAPTURED by rules, especially those of her own making. In the beginning, her rules were simple enough to remember. She had told the other girls: when visiting Madeleine, one must have very clean hands. One must bring her small gifts, such as ribbons or nosegays. When one approaches, the eyes are lowered, the lips whispering, Hush. Then, if you are old enough, and pretty, you might be allowed to arrange her hair on the pillowcase, or stroke her temples with your fingertips. While younger girls should prepare themselves by standing nearby and murmuring, How beautiful.

Now that I think about it, Beatrice had said, you had better practice on me first. That way, if you make any mistakes, I can correct you.

Touch me there, she recommends. And speak more softly. Ow! she complains. You must be more careful. And when you hurt me, you should make up for it with kisses.

The girls listen, and obey. But try as they might, they never seem to master the rules. Someone inevitably laughs; or a pair of fingers gets tangled in Beatrice's hair—all accidents, merely. But this is why practice is necessary, and punishment, too. You must turn ten somersaults. You must be tied to that tree. You must take off your dress and run around in a circle, singing.

And then, the girls ask, gasping and aglow, will you let us see Madeleine?

But even this question forms its own mysterious rule, the girls asking out of neither curiosity nor need but simply habit, in a game where one rule begets another at a pace so dizzying that the outcome has altogether ceased to matter.

recognition

ARE YOU CERTAIN that's me? Madeleine asks, examining the photograph: an unsmiling child punishing a naked man.

The photographer coats a glass plate with collodion; he nods, abstractedly.

When you disappear behind the camera, I tell my eyes: look forgiving. I tell my mouth: appear noble. Where does she go, the person who is forgiving and noble and tender?

Adrien, feeding the plate into the dark maw of his box, says, I'm simply taking your picture.

The me in this photograph is not me, the girl insists. She is Madeleine's ghost, pinned here to the paper.

Adrien lurches dangerously; his equipment sways: Are you ready?

But his subject is not satisfied: Who is that person in the picture?

One, two, three, Adrien counts.

Is there another child out there, sulky and cruel, whom you have accidentally captured in your photograph? And is her name Madeleine?

at the edge of the drive

A LONG DRIVE curves through the estate; it is covered with gravel. When the gypsies first arrived, the wheels of their caravans made a great crunching sound. But the drive has been silent for some time, now; it seems that no one comes and no one leaves; no visitors, no deliveries; nothing interrupts the dream-tedium of days folding in upon themselves, as contortionists do, here on the estate of the widow.

Madeleine rakes the gravel into the dustpan of her hands. By tying her spare drawers at the knees, she has turned them into a sack. As she trudges across the lawn, lugging her drawers behind her, Charlotte sticks her head out from a caravan and says, That looks terribly heavy.

It is! Madeleine replies.

She makes several trips. She remains mysterious.

But she cannot resist, in the midst of her labors, observing to Charlotte: I like to sleep when it's raining outside.

atop a caravan

THE STARS AND MOON do not seem any closer, but the ground looks much farther away, and the roofs of caravans more precarious than expected. Madeleine teeters above the world like a small, drunken seraph. Everyone but she is sleeping.

From below, she hears a moan, a low and plaintive sound rising up through the rooftop, through the soles of her bare feet. M. Pujol is moaning in his sleep, and when she hears this, the sound of loss, Madeleine thrusts her hands deep into her drawers, which she has dragged, with some difficulty, up to these heights.

A fistful of gravel rains down on the caravan.

The moaning ceases, abruptly.

It is just as she predicted! In the darkness, Madeleine glows. And though to her ears the noise is not of raindrops, but simply of gravel rattling across a tin roof, she knows that from below, from the tousled, sheet-tangled bed, the flatulent man hears the sound of rain, and is quieted.

Go to sleep, M. Pujol! she whispers.

Again she digs into her sack.

help

BETWEEN CLOUDBURSTS, Madeleine hears the wobble of wheels being rolled across the lawn. She peers down into the dark, indignantly: Who else is awake?

It is the photographer, who stumbles about during the night as he does during the day, like a somnambulist. He looks up at her and staggers forward, pulling behind him the wagon that holds his photographic equipment. Either he is very tired, or else the load is very heavy.

You should be in bed! Madeleine hisses. It's too late to be taking pictures!

The photographer shuffles on, without heeding her, his forehead gleaming dimly. When he reaches the foot of the caravan, and Madeleine leans over the edge of the roof to shoo him away, she sees that the wagon has been emptied of its canisters, bellows, and bulbs. She sees that the wagon has been filled, instead, with gravel. He has come to help.

This was my idea! hisses Madeleine, from the rooftop.

on the carpet

LOUDER, SAYS THE WIDOW, cupping her hand around her ear.

recognition

BUT ALREADY he has leapt up, swung through the air, attached himself like a wayward trapezist to the tin roof of the caravan. He dangles there, looking glumly up at Madeleine, and she sees that his face is innocent, as if his every gesture, every act, has been performed without his knowledge.

Madeleine steps on his fingers, so she can feel how they tremble from the effort of clutching onto the roof. If only she were heavier. If only he would fall.

Ow, Adrien says.

Her cold toes curl around his knuckles.

Don't, he says.

Her toenails press into the backs of his hands.

This hurts, he says.

And, in saying so, nearly upsets her gravity. Oh yes: this hurts. That which has remained unknown to Madeleine now makes its sudden and forceful acquaintance. It is the sight of dumb, suffering Adrien, it is his small cry, that awakes her.

fall

DOWN SHE PLUMMETS, her drawers sailing out behind her like the skirts of a disaffected angel, or the tail of a plunging kite.

cursed

ADRIEN TAKES THIS OPPORTUNITY to heave himself onto the roof. From the damp ground below, Madeleine scowls at him, thinks up curses. May your every picture be pornographic! May your glass plates shatter! May you ruin every single thing you touch.

Her curses are bitter, not only because he is up on the caravan, and she down on the grass, but also because what was once faint and without name—no more than a shudder, a flush, a short spell of light-headedness, an intestinal fluttering—feels now like a wound.

Without knowing it, he has told Madeleine her own secret.

That she loves the flatulent man; that she aches for him.

declaration

I LOVE YOU, Mother says, in an experimental mood.

The sleeping girl says nothing in return.

Mother puts down her spoon, rubs her hands on her apron, and goes to stand alongside the bed. With a brisk, unthinking movement, she straightens the coverlet so that all is smooth.

She tries again.

I love you, Mother says. Very much.

And the girl, who has been known to sigh enormously, and moan, and even to let loose a ripping snore, makes no sound at all. She is as pale and unresponsive as a lump of dough.

Do you remember, Mother asks, how I used to brush your hair? You would make a rumbling sound in the bottom of your throat, just like a little cat. In the evening, when I sat down with the sewing, you would kneel at my feet and push your head in my lap, seeking out my hands, wanting again the feel of me moving the brush against your scalp. And never once did I not put my needle down and touch you. For it was a pleasure to me, to hear that sound you would make. . . .

In her bed, the girl remains silent, and unmoved.

Do you remember, Mother asks, the story I used to tell you? About the donkey, and the princess, and how she found the golden key. . . .

But Mother finds she can no longer recall the details exactly, nor the ending, nor the plot.

Well, there was a story, she says, and what matters is that you liked it, and that I told it to you. I told it to you countless times, for you could not be satisfied, and would refuse to hear another story, or to hear the story told by any other voice but mine. So I told it, again and again, long after I had grown sick of it, because you wanted to hear my voice, repeating the words that pleased you. Do you remember that? Do you remember my voice?

And, leaning very close to the pillow, so close that she can feel the moistness of her daughter's breath, she says, again, I love you.

The sleeping girl does not so much as shudder.

Ach, Madeleine! Mother cries in despair, turning away from the bed. You were always stubborn!

mutiny

SMACK! IS THE SOUND of the girl's hand falling squarely upon the backside of M. Pujol. *Smack!* is the sound of her palm meeting the flesh of his bared cheeks.

Tonight, though, the widow hears nothing. No sound at all. She leans forward, frowning, in her delicate chair. She cups a hand around her ear.

As M. Pujol twists his head over his left shoulder, Adrien steps out from beneath his shroud, and Charlotte lifts her fingers from her strings. They all look at Madeleine, who is wincing and wagging her hand, as if from the sting of a very sharp blow.

At last she declares: The widow has gone completely deaf!

The performers stare at her effrontery. Hasn't the widow just complained of M. Pujol's sighs, and punished the servants for singing in the kitchen?

I am not in the least deaf, the widow says.

All but Madeleine nod slowly in agreement.

Leaning back in her chair, the widow says, Why not try again.

But Madeleine's paddles are now fists, and her arms hang stiff at her sides like two furious exclamation marks.

No, she says.

She is obstinacy itself.

iron maiden

THE WIDOW SMILES at Madeleine, and rising from her seat, gestures for the girl to follow.

Together they disappear inside the widow's chambers, where the drapery falls behind them with the soft, deadly sound of snow sliding off a roof. The last thing the performers see is Madeleine's scornful glance, trained on them as she turns back, before the curtains envelop her: You are cowardly, all of you, she remonstrates. I had a plan!

In silence the performers imagine terrible things. No one has ever entered the private rooms of the widow.

in the chambers of the widow

THE CURTAINS OPEN onto a darkened hallway, so dark that she must run her fingertips along the walls, and at the end of it, there are more curtains, as dense and velvety as the first. Then there is a warm room, with walls the color of pomegranates, where she is given toast with raisins, told to take off her shoes, placed before the fire on a footstool. And above her, on the mantelpiece, is a miniature circus made all of tin, with its stiff pennants flying and its elephants parading.

Am I too old for this, Madeleine wonders, because she would like to touch it, to see if the lion tamer's arms move in his sockets, or if there is a key she can turn, releasing music.

She would also like to unbutton the dress of the waxy doll standing aloof in the corner; slide her hands over the sad, long face of the wooden horse; ask for two more pieces of toast. Then she remembers: I am in trouble. Also: I can neither button nor unbutton.

But the widow does not seem angry in the least. When she speaks, it is in a coaxing and conspiratorial tone that Madeleine is startled to recognize, and all at once the pull of the horse, the perfect circus, becomes stronger: for the widow—of course— is a grandmother, and these belong to her grandchildren, and Madeleine is not indifferent to the strange magnetism exercised by other children's things.

beatific

THE WIDOW SAYS: I, too, feel sympathy for M. Pujol.

Madeleine studies her toast. There are three raisins remaining, clustered like a birthmark, and the crust, which isn't burnt.

The widow says, So you must not think that I am unfriendly.

Is it better to take many small bites, that taste almost of nothing, or to devour it all at once, and feel regret?

The widow persists, I might even understand why you won't do as I ask.

Crunch. Then no more.

Is it perhaps because, the widow ventures, you have fallen—

The crust catches on its way down. Madeleine turns colors, throws her fist against her chest.

He reminds me of my favorite saint, she gasps.

Who is your favorite? the widow asks. Let me guess, she adds, leaning closer: Sebastian.

Saint Michel, Madeleine says, recovered. In the cathedral, in my town, there is a picture of him in the window. M. Pujol looks exactly like him, except M. Pujol wears a moustache.

And remembering what they taught her at the convent, she folds her paddles neatly in her lap.

But unlike Michel, the widow says, M. Pujol has not been restored to his former beauty and perfection. He remains wretched.

So the widow is familiar with the excesses of the saints.

And for that reason, she murmurs, you wish to spare him.

Madeleine nods. She believes herself saved.

For the widow has turned her back to Madeleine, as though in deference to her argument, and is now fingering the small figures on her mantelpiece. From her stool, Madeleine contemplates her own piety.

Very softly, the widow says: You are mistaken.

And whispering to the tiny circus, she says: He moans like a man in pain. But what you must understand is that you comfort him with your blows.

Turning towards Madeleine, she hands her the lion tamer in his tight scarlet trousers. Madeleine grips him unsafely in her mitts and discovers it is true: his arms move, as do his well-shaped legs, and his head; all of him moves, with terrible pliancy. Even his wrist, flicking his tiny lash, twists on an invisible screw.

You are attending to his wounds, the widow murmurs. You are ministering, with your maimed hands, to his every suffering.

Inside Madeleine something trembles, then falls into place with a thud.

Like the abbot at Rievaulx, she says dully.

The plash of water in a bowl, the wringing of cloths—

Exactly, says the widow, who again offers her lovely smile, and places her hand lightly upon Madeleine's head: You are filled with kindness.

unlike

IT IS RARE that the widow experiences surprise. But when the girl leaps from the stool, threatening the teacups, and gnaws her lips in agony, and roughly returns the lion tamer to the mantelpiece, his limbs all askew, and at last announces—I am not like the abbot—careless of how she strews crumbs everywhere, the widow is taken aback.

I am more like Michel, the girl says, before she struggles her way into the heavy curtains, without waiting to be dismissed. Michel! she shrieks, with all the fury and astonishment of one usurped.

shrubbery

THE PRIEST ADDRESSES his flock with affection.

My children, he says, and feels a sudden strange yearning of heart, for indeed they are like children, stirring in their seats, nudging the warm sides of their neighbors, marking time, he is sure, through all manner of small devices. See how the chemist, with his bemused expression, calculates the amount of emetic he should order in the coming week. The mayor's lips barely move as he rehearses the difficult conversation he must have with his daughter. While the captain of the gendarmes, he closes his eyes and dreams.

But the girls—look at them—their concentration is ferocious. They nod over their prayer books. Their heads touch. They follow the words with their fingers. How sober, and upright, and fine they appear, like a stand of young trees growing in the midst of untended shrubbery. They are the first to echo him: Amen. Their low, sweet voices sound all at once, in perfect agreement.

prayer

BENEATH BEATRICE'S FINGER: the word Handmaid.
   And then: Unto.
   Her finger drifts to the bottom of the page: Shall.
   And rests upon the word: House.
   H-U-S-H, Sophie spells, shivering in her excitement.

hush

BEHIND THE HEAVY CURTAINS, all is quiet. Madeleine pauses, there at the end of the passageway, and listens: where is the sound of Charlotte's bow, tapping absently against the floor, and the murmur of Marguerite's disparagements? The swish of stockinged feet, the clanking of canisters against the little wagon, and the sigh of the drawing-room windows being pulled shut after the last cigarette has been flicked onto the lawn? The secret, languid sound of the performers laughing, unobserved?

Madeleine had hoped to burst through the curtains, ablaze with her anger, frightening the others and making them feel small. They would freeze; they would stare at her. They would be struck, as if with Marguerite's wooden sword, by the sight of Madeleine, enraged.

So she had thought as she came rushing down the hall. But now she halts, uncertain, thwarted by this peculiar silence. Not a silence, exactly; a peculiar hush: for it does not sound as if the drawing room is empty, but rather that those inside have grown suddenly quiet. Madeleine gets the uncomfortable feeling that were she to enter, were she to throw back the drapery and storm through, it would be an intrusion.

audience

WITH MADELEINE, though, curiosity prevails, always.

And so the curtain is lifted.

Behold: the flatulent man is nearly dressed. No longer on his hands and knees, he wears his black satin breeches, his elegant tailcoat. His fingers fumble in the stiff white folds of his butterfly tie. The others have grown tired of waiting, perhaps, and wandered off to bed. This seems an unexpected gift to Madeleine, that he should be alone, that she should be allowed to watch him as he dresses, to love his fastidiousness, to picture him as he once stood: upright, clothed, framed by a scarlet curtain. She imagines the dimming of lights, ushers disappearing, programs rustling, an old gentleman coughing, and the breathless heavenly feeling that yes, yes, it is all about to begin. . . .

But then another player stumbles out from the wings. His face wears the dismayed expression of someone who finds himself in the wrong production. He looks back over his shoulder beseechingly, as if a stagehand might whisper his lines, or a tremendous piece of scenery might roll out and flatten him beneath its wheels. How did I end up here? his whole body asks, twitching in the candlelight, longing to do away with itself.

The flatulent man makes a small, exasperated noise. His arms drop to his sides.

Upstaged, once again, by an amateur. His triumphant return, foiled!

reveal

NO; HE IS HAVING DIFFICULTY with his butterfly tie.

And suddenly Adrien seems to remember what it is that he is supposed to do. His eyes brighten; he steps forward with courage; he lifts his arm and—like that—it falls away from him, his clumsiness and coarseness and bewilderment, it all falls away, like the sleeve of a dressing gown as a young woman raises her hand to brush her hair, exposing the whiteness of her forearm, her elbow— like that, his purpose is revealed, that beautifully. He must fix the flatulent man's tie. And his face no longer resembles that of the sleepwalker, or the opium eater; his face is that of a man who must tilt M. Pujol's chin, with all the tenderness in the world, and arrange the wing-like folds of his white evening tie.

metamorphosis

SHE LETS THE CURTAIN FALL. She stands there in the darkness, panting.

Memory will not adjust to this: the pulse, the stirring, of new organs. Her desire draws out its feelers, and unfolds its sticky wings.

transfixed

NEVER—NOT WHEN the prince kissed the princess, nor the priest laid the host upon one's tongue, not when Madeleine gripped the despondent member of M. Jouy, nor when Papa held Maman in the dark, not the brothers and sisters pressing their small, hot hands against the sleeping girl—has a person touched another with such tender concentration.

And in his touch there is not the kindness, the abnegation, of the abbot tending to the wounded Michel: here, there are no ministrations, no saints; no blazing suns, no attendant moons. There is only this perfect reciprocity—two stars in orbit, two flowers unfolding—an exchange of pleasure unlike that she has ever seen.

She watches how his fingers float over the crooked tie, the pale throat, the apple bumping along its narrow path, and it is as if this gesture has never before existed, has only now been invented by dint of his hunger. He must teach his hands, his fingers, to do that which is utterly strange to them. And to defy habit in this way— what force is great enough? How shabby, how halfhearted, her own mutiny now seems. So what force? Madeleine does not know. She knows only that the sight of it could impale her. That she could part the curtains and watch, swooning, as the gesture is performed again and again.

overture

AND SO THE CURTAIN is lifted.

As she looks once more on the scene inside, she thinks of a violinist tucking his instrument beneath his chin.

Behold: M. Pujol is pressing his cheek upon the photographer's hand. The hand is resting, like a violin, against his collarbone. He does not rub his cheek against the hand, as though it were the rabbit trimming on a coat, nor does he dig his chin into the flesh, like a half-wit who wants nothing more than to sink his face into the warmth of his own shoulder. He simply holds the hand against him, and in his touch is the impatience with which musicians handle their instruments.

He closes his eyes. He takes a breath.

It is all about to begin.

interrupted

THEN, IN HER EMOTION, in her extreme but vague excitement, it happens—Madeleine makes a wheezing sound. If there is a nestling in her hands, she will fondle it to death. If there is a reflection in a pool, she will peer too closely, lose her balance, splash through it with her boots. Her rough hands, her muddy boots, and the wings thrashing savagely inside her, sending up this wheeze, this strange whistling sound.

The hand retreats. The two men step away from each other. They look about them slowly, blinking sleepily like children.

To her relief, to her anguish, they do not see her.

invisible

THEY DO NOT SEE ME! Claude rejoices, silently. For everything about him now is silent: his thoughts, his beating heart, his footfalls in the underbrush. He can tiptoe past all sorts of doors and nobody inside would know it. He seems to be mastering invisibility as well, for look: how close to the girls he crouches! So close that if he were to sneeze and not cover his mouth, they would each of them feel, on their necks and their cheeks, a satiny mist, like one coming off the sea. Claude is that close to them. He has crept there silently. His invisible body trembles in its joy and proximity.

It will be his at last, the secret. He alone will know what happens when the girls all disappear. For a moment, in the underbrush, he imagines how he will raise his hand, and stand, and issue a statement, or file a report. He imagines the magisterial weight of approval, the heaviness of men's palms clapping him on the shoulder. But then, easing a ticklish branch to one side, he pictures another possibility: that of nursing his secret, hiding it from sight, taking it out in the dark and stroking it, keeping it for the enjoyment of Claude alone.

But how to get that meaty one to move—her hips now occupy the whole of his view. As she sways back and forth in her eagerness, he catches only slivers of what he wants to see, which is maybe more maddening than not being able to see at all, and certainly more exciting than being able to see everything at once. He glimpses a pair of tentative hands, reaching out; a scattering, on pale skin, of petals; the flash of a mirror in the sunlight; the pucker of a navel. Could that be right? Naked skin? A belly button?

little jug

THE MAYOR CLEARS his throat. He pushes aside his plate. He regards his youngest daughter, who is chewing her bread enthusiastically, and not giving him any encouragement at all.

I am an indulgent father, he begins. Which is a fine beginning; which is what he rehearsed. Firstly: his affectionate nature and dislike of tyranny; secondly: his public obligations; thirdly: the strange reports that have lately reached him, of sightings, and silences, and the odd, glittering look in his youngest daughter's eye, the bits of grass seen caught in her hair; and fourthly: he cannot remember fourthly.

Emma, he says.

And notices, as he often does, the stubbiness of her fingers. It would be quite impossible to pry those fingers from anything they might decide to grasp. One day, he expects, they will lengthen into cool, slender, white fingers, from which will issue all sorts of gentle touches and the pretty, even handwriting that he sees on invitations. As it stands, her lettering is heavy on the page, and executed with the same methodical relish with which she is now sawing off another piece of bread. But yes, her fingers will lengthen, and her complexion will not be so swarthy, and little curlicues will bloom upon the barren slopes of her alphabet.

Emma, he says again, and because her mouth is full, she reaches across the table and squeezes his hand. Yes, Papa, I am listening, is what her stubby fingers say. With warmth, and great insistence; and what a very pleasant feeling it is to be gripped by such fingers, and to know that nothing could ever tear you from their hold. The mayor finds himself thinking that perhaps it would not be so terrible were his daughter to remain always like this: this small, this brown and sturdy, like a jug.

I am an indulgent father, he repeats, helplessly, and he can go no further.

apprehended

THE MAYOR'S ELDEST DAUGHTER is more to the point. Circling around the table, dishes balanced dangerously in one hand, she sees a butter knife making its way towards the jar of preserves.

Aha! she cries, grabbing with her free hand her sister's brown wrist, the butter knife flashing wildly like a fish twisting in a beak.

Let go, Emma says. I'm still eating.

No, her sister says. You let go. Let go of the knife.

But Emma is not yet finished with her breakfast. She would like to spread some jam on her last piece of bread. If she cannot spread her jam, like a lady, she will simply have to dunk her crust into the jar itself. So, forgetting the knife, she reaches out to grasp the lovely, golden, glowing jar that sings its siren song from across the table.

The eldest daughter perceives with alarm the younger's intent. The cutlery clatters, the dishes sway.

Take these!

The mayor finds himself responsible for the china.

And still pinching the brown wrist in one hand, his eldest daughter confiscates the treacherous jampot. She holds it up above her head, away from the clamorous hands of her sister, and looks down, as if from a great height, at her father's puzzled face.

Don't you see? she asks.

tell me

YOU MUST SEE, the photographer pleads. You must see how you are—compromising—

His hands fly up from his pockets, fluttering with urgency, making all the arguments that language has failed to provide him with. Madeleine notes this carefully, the articulateness of his hands. He has become, quite suddenly, interesting to her. She grows shy in his presence. She is curious about everything he does.

Wrecking? Madeleine asks, as his hands wring the air. Destroying?

Together they stand at the edge of the lawn. She is spreading her newly washed drawers across the privet hedge to dry. How white they appear against the green, looking as if they might rise up at any moment, like sails, and pull with them the privet hedge, the velvety lawns, the grand house with its carpets and curtains. Only a great gust of wind is needed, and all will be unmoored.

Madeleine must concentrate on this, the white against the green, so as not to gaze too long at the photographer's face, or his talkative hands.

Yes, Adrien admits, exhausted. You are destroying everything.

He means that the widow is unhappy. She is unhappy because the girl continues to refuse her. Every night, they gather in her drawing room; every night, the candles are lit, the tripod's spindly legs are spread, the performers are placed in their humiliating poses; every night, the girl lifts her paddle (his cheek, her hand, *smack!* was the sound) and freezes.

Madeleine nods, pretends to listen. She would like to be having a different conversation. She would like to ask, Do you chew anise seeds? And is that you I hear sometimes, singing beneath your breath? Maybe they could take a turn around the garden. Maybe he could invite her inside, for a drink of water. What gives your shirts their nice smell? She wants to say, Tell me. She wants to know: Was it like—? Did you feel—?

She will send us away, the photographer says.

taste

SPECIAL DELIVERY! Mother sings out, clutching a jar in each of her hands.

But the mayor opens his door no more than a crack.

Mother smiles at him shyly. It's pear, she says. Your favorite.

The crack widens by a hair.

Madame, the mayor begins, I am a supporter of local business—

Indeed you are! she cries. Last month you bought a dozen jars!

And presenting her gifts, she says, Do not think I have forgotten.

The door creeps farther open, then closes with a slam.

Mother stumbles backwards. She stares at the mayor's front door; she frowns at this most uncivic display.

The red door swings open once again. The mayor has been replaced by his sour-faced daughter, her jaw set, her feet planted. Old enough, Mother thinks, to be married by now, and bullying someone other than her father.

Good morning, Mother ventures.

What do you want? the daughter replies.

To leave a token, Mother says, of my appreciation for the mayor.

And she holds up each golden specimen for her to see.

Preserves! the daughter snorts. Just as I thought!

She folds her arms across her narrow chest: We are not interested. The things you make—they have a queer taste.

Mother, looking in dismay at her jars, cannot muster a reply. The mayor's daughter takes advantage. She observes, as she closes for the last time the door, But why should you care whether we like your preserves? You have so many customers in *Paris.*

naps

THE FLATULENT MAN is very tired. His pale face has turned grey. Two dark circles seep from beneath his eyes, like drops of ink dissolving in a bowl of milk.

It is necessary now to take naps. Every afternoon he goes off hunting for them. Sometimes he is lucky: once, behind the gatehouse, in a cool damp spot that smelled of clay; another time, in a corner of the kitchen garden, abandoned to the eggplants. He creeps up on these places. He makes himself thin as a shadow.

When he wakes, he expects to find himself squinting into the sun. He expects that a long afternoon has passed, that the sun has moved across the sky and found him, its light slanting across his face, staining the inside of his eyelids. So he is surprised, when he wakes, to discover himself still in shadow, to see only the green sweating flagstone of the gatehouse, its surface alive with insects; or the dark, hairy depths of the tomato vines. And when he draws himself up onto his elbows, he will often hear a rustling, will catch a glimpse of white stocking disappearing into the foliage, or the flash of a silver watch chain.

He wants to cry out, Wait!

But the two are doe-like creatures; they seek him out and stare, then flee, their white tails showing. They spring off into the underbrush, off to their quarrels, their little anxious tasks, their acts of love, before he can stop them and say: At night, with the gravel rattling overhead—I have difficulty sleeping.

poem

LOOKING AT HIM, the man asleep in the garden, Adrien says, One time I touched his face.

Madeleine, at his elbow, finds her eyes watering at the thought of this.

He offers her the nice-smelling sleeve of his shirt.

Can you see? he asks, pushing aside a branch, pushing the hair from her face.

The sight makes her suffer. There he is, her enemy, on the ground as if dead: he who has, without knowing, without even trying, replaced her in her own affections. This makes the concession all the more galling to her, this unconsciousness. Yet the beauty of him asleep, arm thrown out, mouth open—if only she knew a poem! If only her hands and fingers could speak for her, making eloquent shapes in the air as Adrien's do. It is with one of these fingers that he tucks a piece of hair behind her ear. She turns to him, full of speech. But her hands are struck dumb, and the only words that occur to her are: Orchard. Swallow. Bell.

mise en scène

M. PUJOL KNOWS what he will find when he opens the drawing-room door. He pictures it with the same sense of misgiving with which he recalls the schoolroom he sat in when he was a child, the map he had drawn of its dangers and unfriendly territories: the desk with an obscene picture on its lid; the alcove where the strongest boys hatched their plots; the row of meek children who would look at him knowingly, as if he belonged to them; the chair with the mysterious words scratched under its seat, over the ridges of which he would trace his fingers helplessly, and then pull his hands away in self-disgust, feeling contaminated. He had been glad, as a child, to be taken from that schoolroom. It was all thanks to his unusual gift.

But what now could deliver him?

Deliver him from the constellation of widow, girl, photographer: one perched on the edge of her delicate chair, one waiting at attention on the carpet, one crouched behind his camera, making the whole contraption tremble with his hunger. In a corner of the drawing room stands an Oriental screen, behind which he will be asked to take off his clothes. In another corner is a small bust of Racine. In the window seat is Marguerite, pouring lotion from a bottle into the thick palm of her hand. And crowded against each other, limbs and haunches bumping, like statuary forgotten in a warehouse, are the acrobats, the emaciated man, the dog girl, and the stringed woman, each body arranged to tell its own story.

knight

IF HE DECLINED TO open the door, if he refused to enter—would that be cowardly or brave? Trusting habit, he should think himself a coward. But when he stands outside the drawing-room door, his damp forehead resting against the frame, he discovers that what he fears most is not his own humiliation, which he has grown used to, but rather the fury that will be unleashed upon the girl. And to rescue her—that would be a brave thing. What a brave thing! For the girl, in her stubbornness, is met every night with glowering looks, and pinches, and the thump of the acrobats as they collapse accusingly onto the carpet. Sometimes Marguerite rises up from the window seat and strikes her. As for the widow, she never shows her displeasure, but the very restraint with which she leaves the room makes him afraid.

He could save her from this, he thinks, by his absence. It would be as simple as leaving. As simple as airing out his travelling case, folding his evening clothes in tissue paper, sliding his shoes into their little felt bags, putting his brushes in order. How easy and how courageous it would be, to leave. He imagines how the gravel will crunch underfoot, the feel of his case bumping against his side. A flying leap! An adventure! But where to? That he will consider later. For now, as he nods to Racine, as he disappears behind the Oriental screen, his fingers already loosening his white evening tie, he will think only of the felted bags, soft and grey and consoling as the moles he sometimes finds outside his door, in the mornings.

arcane

WHAT A BRAVE THING he is about to do! M. Pujol swells; feels briefly, blissfully, free from disgrace. But as he looks up at her, it occurs to him that the girl does not lend herself very well to being saved: she is too odd, too refractory; she looks unsettling as she stands there, paddle suspended, and even when Marguerite's ivory fan cracks against the side of her head, the girl's face remains furrowed in thought. Though dressed as she is, ridiculously, in a froth of petticoats and bows, there is nothing she resembles more than a fading scholar, lost within the thickets of his own peculiar field. The ivory fan makes a sharp and terrible noise, yet she looks as though she is deciphering a moldy text, or perhaps creeping her way through a mathematical proof.

archaeology

WHEN SHE GAZES AT HIS BODY, crouching on the carpet, the only words that occur to her are: Orchard. Swallow. Bell.

One morning her father found in their field a ruined coin. In the very place where he stood was once a town, but then an empire collapsed and the buildings languished and the river overflowed its banks, flooding everything. This is what she imagines. How else does a town sink into the earth? It lies buried far below, where all is dark and still, but on occasion some small thing will loose itself from the town and feel its way to the surface. Her father found a coin. Another man found a bottle. If it were not for the coin, and the bottle, they would not have believed that a town existed.

She hears the word bell, or orchard, or swallow, and she experiences a strange surprise, like the feel of a coin in the soil. These words make her wistful; they overwhelm her with longing. Not for her orchard, nor the bell in her church, nor the swallows that nest in the eaves of her house. For something else altogether, something she would have forgotten completely.

She wonders: Why should these words pierce me, if they are not the remains of a currency I once knew how to spend?

in the candlelight

CRACK! IS THE SOUND of an ivory fan meeting the furred curve of a child's ear.

unclean

BRUISES BEGIN TO RISE upon the skin of the sleeping girl. All
over her body bloom patches of lavender and gold and lichen green.
Beatrice conducts a concerned examination: What could be the
cause of this?

Mother hunkers over her cauldron, saying nothing. She thinks,
Sometimes I grow clumsy with the handle of the broom. But is it
my fault, that she takes up so much space?

The preserves seethe about the neck of her spoon. Drops of
sweat tremble on her brow. She frowns down, protectively, at the
mess she has concocted: she must devise a defense. Her business,
which she has nurtured so very tenderly, now finds itself under
attack.

The other women of the village, who until this point have been
her stalwart companions, her confederates, her sisters-in-arms, have
risen up against her. The reason? Covetousness, simply, which is
certainly a sin. They begrudge her the success that has struck her
house, swift and unbidden as the lightning bolt that set the mayor's
roof on fire. The new fur muff in her lap, the lustrous flanks of her
new horse, the rattle of the jam jars atop the postman's cart: it all
feeds their fury. Sabotage is their only recourse, and soon rumors
of unwholesomeness and sorcery are set roaming about the streets.

Shattered crocks appear on her doorstep; the stone wall is
speckled with jam. One day, on her way to market, she sees that
a shrill placard has been erected along the road:

IF THE FLESH IS UNCLEAN THEN SO IS THE FOOD
BEWARE THE PRODUCTS OF AN UNHOLY HOME!

She turns abruptly and stomps her way home. There, she surveys the girl spread before her, dewy and white and unruffled: You are the source of all this trouble, Mother says.

deal

M. PUJOL CAN SEE the girl and the photographer, quarrelling once more behind the shrubbery. A flurry of fingers rises up above the privet hedge. If he stood his travelling case on one end, and climbed on top, he could wave his arms; he could cry out, Adrien! and maybe the photographer would turn around and slowly smile. But instead he drives a bargain with himself: I will not call out his name, as long as—above him an arbiter rustles, presents itself— that leaf does not fall from that tree.

He repeats the terms. They seem fair. And trusting in the impartial justice of the universe, he sits down on his travelling case.

The voices continue, passing from reproach to lament to something he cannot quite recognize. Please. His face. Cannot. I saw you. The words sift over and stain him like pollen: Your hands. I cannot. But then a wind rises and the leaves stir and the voices are carried in the opposite direction, away from him. Remembering his leaf, he is sent into a panic: so many of them! All rustling, shifting, silvering; made unrecognizable in their commotion. But eventually the wind subsides and the leaves are stilled and once more it is revealed: his leaf, the one not as green as the others; looking, in fact, somewhat sickly. It trembles on its stem. It twists fretfully against the sky. When the wind lifts again, so do the flatulent man's hopes.

But the leaf is more firmly attached to the tree than, by all appearances, it should be.

M. Pujol searches for other signs: If that crow takes flight, he tells himself. That thistle bursts. That handsaw, in the distance, ceases.

Then I will not have to go.

harbinger

THERE WAS ANOTHER young man once, his father an ambassador to a country M. Pujol had never heard of. He had come backstage bearing an armful of orchids, of cattleyas, and M. Pujol had shrunk in embarrassment: as though I were an opera dancer! But the young man presented them with his eyes lowered, saying nothing; and M. Pujol felt that to be insulted long would be impossible.

Together they spoke little, and not often of love. Which is perhaps why, when remembering that year, M. Pujol will say of it only, My happiness then cannot be described. He means it literally, but how theatrical it sounds! To hear himself say it, even silently (for no one has asked), makes him prickle with shame. He takes refuge in these facts: the carriage we rode in was green; he had a scar, from an appendix operation, of which he was proud; he attended sixteen of my performances and his enthusiasm did not wane; his name was Hugh.

The year had ended suddenly, with the announcement of his engagement to a young lady with two houses in Neuilly, near the Bois de Boulogne. At the time M. Pujol had found it painful to accept the news, but looking back he sees that it was simply the portent of what was to come. So that when, many months later, he would once again lose what he loved most to an ordinary woman— La Femme-Petomane!—the shock would not be too great for him.

signs

BUT THE PHOTOGRAPHER is unlikely to marry a woman with houses. He seems to have few prospects at all, of any kind. He lacks coordination; he tries to but cannot grow a moustache; his pictures are of an uneven quality. When he speaks, he has trouble looking one in the eye. But his hand had not trembled. What a surprise that had been: a most touching surprise.

The whole world is bent on surprising M. Pujol. There is a conspiracy afoot, it seems, a conspiracy to gratify him. From the far field comes a cracking, a whistling, and after that, silence; the handsaw is now abandoned in the grass, the task completed, and as if startled by the cessation of that gnawing sound, the crow shakes its wings and takes to the air, and as if released, at last, by the little spring with which the crow leaves its perch, the branch shudders, the leaves quiver, and a sickly yellow specimen comes spinning down from the sky.

The flatulent man looks about him in astonishment. Could the universe be capable of such kindness? Clambering atop his travelling case, he clears his throat; he prepares a greeting; he wonders if to wave his arms would throw off his balance.

He will cry out, Adrien! and the young man will turn around and look at him.

But oh, surprise: the stern Impossible! The photographer is no longer there. The crown of his head does not float above the privet hedge, nor do his pale frantic fingers. Nothing of him remains visible; he has sunk beneath the privet hedge like a ship, or a sun. M. Pujol, stranded on his travelling case, is left to search the horizon and wonder. He was just here, he protests. How could I have lost him?

substitute

IF YOU WERE M. Pujol, Madeleine says, I would reach out my hand to you. Like this.

If you were M. Pujol, Adrien says, I would press my mouth against your pulse. Like this.

If you were he, she says, I would cup your chin in my fingers.

If you were he, he says, I would take those fingers into my mouth.

Then my mouth would envy my fingers, she says.

Then your mouth must usurp your fingers, he says.

And then, she says, I would do this.

hunter

FROM HER WINDOW, high above the world, the widow spots them, the child and her photographer, entangled in the shadows of the shrubbery. And as she watches them, she feels the briefest flicker, like the singe of a match tip's flame: quickly, now, before it's gone! She tugs upon the bell rope that dangles beside her: a photograph must be taken; the moment must not be lost. Yes, here is the hind of her nighttime hunts; she has tracked it down at last.

Then she laughs at herself, at the futility of her agitated summons. For how can he take the picture, when he is the picture? All of her efforts, if she is to be truthful, are marked by this same sense of impossibility. The more furiously she pursues, the more surely it recedes, this fugitive scene, visible only when glimpsed askance, out of the corner of her rheumy eye. Her latest project has been a failure; she had hoped that this marvelous invention, this alchemy of chemicals and light, would assist her in her pursuits, but now, as her eyes graze over the photographs, she discovers that they offer her nothing. And if they do, it is only by accident: in one picture, the fringe of the carpet is caught between the man's toes; in another, the child's mouth is open, as if she is about to speak: these are the details that prick her. But they are scarce among this series of tableaux, lovingly arranged, though ultimately of no poignance or excitement to her.

Once she had been interviewed by a scientist, who was anxious to include a grandmother in his study of libertines, already several volumes long. He had amused her with the exacting nature of his questions, and his demands that she should include even the most scabrous details in her accounts. She had teased him, she couldn't help it, so strenuous were his attempts to manage her perversions, to render them immobile. What you must finally recognize, she said, what you must understand about my predilections (the scientist leans forward: at long last, the secret!) is that my desire does not take; it turns, as milk does.

For that reason, she feels only a little sad when she finds, slipped beneath her door, a note written in an elegant hand:

Please forgive me. I have left in search of a Faculty of Medicine who might take interest in my unusual condition. I plan to donate my body to Science, so that I can say my life has been of some use to Humankind.

insane

BUT THE CHILD and her photographer are inconsolable. They cleave to each other as orphans do; they seek comfort in the photographs' melancholy caress. Adrien has laid out all his pictures on the grass.

This image, he tells Madeleine, is literally an emanation of M. Pujol: from his body radiates light, which then inscribes itself on the very surface which in turn your gaze now touches.

They find solace only in the certainty that his body still touches them through the medium of light. But it is a solace that, the photographer knows, will lead slowly and inexorably to madness. The pictures before them serve not only as agonizing reminder of his absence but irrefutable proof that he did in fact exist for them, that his skin did burn upon the man's fingertips, that his flesh did shrink from the girl's stinging touch. This proof is what they cannot bear. He was indeed here, the photographs whisper. But he is no longer.

A decision is reached, in the name of sanity. The widow finds beneath her door another note, much less elegantly penned. Two more of her assistants have decamped.

charivari

ALL THE WORLD IS ATREMBLE: the dogs barking, the bells
clanging, the fine white scent of orange blossoms everywhere, and
Jean-Luc scuttling out the door before Mother can do anything
about it. He is off to join the other boys, who are stealing enough
copper pots and pans to deafen the whole town, when tonight they
go marching through the streets, banging and hallooing till the
dawn.

It is in this moment of confusion, with every child in motion
around her, the girls leaning out the windows, waving, and the boys
snatching up her spoons, that Mother looks at Madeleine. How still
she is, how quietly she sleeps. Her breathing barely lifts the covers.

She is so beautiful when she sleeps.

The children stop. They stare at their mother. They have not
heard this said in a very long while.

Smooth your sister's coverlet. Arrange her hair on the
pillowcase.

And Mother gazes at the girl with a calm affection, as if their
silent quarrels were now coming to an end, as if that lush and
troublesome body had been restored, by miracle, to its former
beauty and perfection.

Outside, the church bells cease their clamor. On the stone steps
leading down from the chapel, a bride and groom stand blinking
stupidly in the sunlight.

Why did I never think of it before? Mother wonders.

heavensent

THE TWO TRAVELLERS, sheltering beneath a chestnut tree, are startled by a crashing, a harried thrashing, from above. It is Mme. Cochon, struggling to free herself from the embrace of an amorous upper branch. Her dainty wings churn the air, her stout legs kick furiously, and from a neighboring tree, a wild cloud of sparrows rises up in sisterly agitation.

Mme. Cochon! cries Madeleine, whose earthbound perspective grants her insight into the situation. Your skirts! They are caught!

The enormous woman heaves herself over so that she can unlatch her hem from the tree. Oh, bother, she gasps, this is always happening.

Madeleine, in her excitement, treads upon the photographer's toes. A face from home! It has been so long. She trots backwards and beams up at the woman, whose buttocks bob among the leaves like the hull of a capsized ship. With a crackling of twigs and a fluttering of wings, Mme. Cochon pulls herself upright.

She calls down to Madeleine, Your mother doesn't know what to make of you!

The girl grins back at her: She never did!

Adrien tugs at Madeleine's sleeve: he hopes to take advantage of the fat woman's surprising appendages. From up there, she can see the entire world, or at least a sizeable portion of it.

Mme. Cochon! Madeleine hurls her voice at the sky. Have you seen a tall and pale-faced man pass this way? Carrying a porcelain basin, a length of rubber tubing, a silver candlestick, and a small family of flutes? You would have noticed his elegant costume; he dresses beautifully, no matter what time of day.

The fat woman sails upward, always happy to oblige.

The two travellers wait below, his hand clasping her paw.

A black tailcoat? Mme. Cochon hollers. Satin breeches ruched at the knee?

Oh yes! That's him!

The woman, high above them, points towards the horizon: He is headed for the hospital at Maréville.

the hospital

RISING UP FROM behind a hill, the hospital at Maréville has as
many windows as it does patients; its hundred eyes glitter in the
morning sun. For every patient, a window, floating high above his
head—too high out of which to climb, or even to gaze. When
passing by the hospital, one never sees a crazy face pressed against
the pane. One is never made aware of the hundred lives contained
within. Yet the feeling persists that the building, so modern and
brick and glittering with glass, is animated by a peculiar
intelligence, and that while the rest of the world is sleeping, at
least one of those eyes is still open, and wakeful, and watching.

The hospital eschews all reminders of its past. Do not call it
the madhouse, or the lunatic asylum. All that was once dark and
hidden and misshapen is now frankly examined in the light that
comes streaming, unchecked, through these flashing windows.
It is the Institute for the Study of Aberrant Behaviors and
Conditions. When Madeleine rings at the front gate, a ruddy,
uniformed matron appears, bringing with her the smell of laundry
soap, square meals, sanitary practices. Her glance takes in the girl,
the photographer, the little wagon brimming with canisters and
bellows and bulbs. She spies the crippled hands.

Come in, the matron says. Come in.

request

MOTHER CONSULTS THE CHEMIST, once again. In his opinion, her letter should request M. Jouy's release for reasons of utmost urgency. When writing correspondence of an official nature, he says, it is better to remain vague.

He returns his spectacles to the bald crest of his head.

No mention of marriage? Mother asks.

The officials at Maréville might not approve, he says.

Approve? Mother says. Who are they to approve? They should stick to drawing pictures.

In a distinctly dispirited way, the chemist rearranges his selection of eye droppers.

Nevertheless, he says, the fate of M. Jouy is in their hands, and if you desire him for a son-in-law, you must first arrange for his release from the hospital.

Would it be dishonest, Mother asks, to describe myself as a member of the family?

If I were you, he says, I would prefer the phrase: interested party.

He sees that Mother is about to object.

misapprehended

OH NO, ADRIEN SAYS, ALARMED: We are not here as patients!

Madeleine shakes her head. A terrible mistake is about to be made. The matron waits beside the door, rustling her skirts.

Then why are you here? The director squints at them from across the expanse of his formidable desk.

This is a good question. As the matron ushered them down the gleaming hallways, it became clear to the photographer that rescuing M. Pujol would require a great deal of cleverness and strategy. The wheels of the little wagon had squealed upon the polished floor; a series of doors had stretched far away into the distance. The flatulent man had not, as they expected, been waiting for them in either a tower or a dungeon, rattling his chains and crying out their names.

Well, Adrien says weakly. I am a photographer.

He indicates the wagon resting beside him: I take photographs.

advances

THE DIRECTOR SMILES. Though his eyes are sunken, and his eyebrows overgrown, he has all the eagerness and bloom of a young man. It is he who oversaw the installation of the windows. Besotted with everything that is novel and newfangled, he sees, in the little wagon, the possibility of further innovation.

What do I spend my days in pursuit of? he suddenly asks. I seem to lead a sedentary existence—he flaps his hands at the desk, the matron, the shelves of books—but mine is a life devoted to the chase. Other doctors deal with sickness in all of its physical manifestations: a swollen abdomen, a blistered tongue, a scaly patch of skin. But illness does not always write itself upon the body; the sickness I search for is hidden deep within the brain. Sometimes it rises to the surface. Sometimes the face betrays what the body conceals. But these moments, these betrayals, last no longer than an instant. They come, they go, they pass over the patient, darkening and brightening his face like clouds gusting over a meadow. How is it possible, then, to tell what he is suffering when the visible signs of his inner disorder appear so fleetingly upon his face?

I don't know, says Adrien.

Neither do I, says Madeleine.

Removing himself from behind his desk, the director crouches down beside the wagon. He strokes the black box that sits among the canisters and bellows and bulbs, and his touch is reverent, as if the box might abruptly snatch off the first joints of his fingers.

One science, he says, in aid of another.

You, he says to Adrien, can capture that which I so hotly pursue.

Adrien fails to understand.

You will take pictures! the director says. You will photograph my patients. Their symptoms will show themselves in your photographs.

Adrien nods, mystified.

But who, the director asks, and stares at Madeleine, is she?

My valuable assistant, the photographer answers, as Madeleine slips her hands beneath her thighs.

aroused

AFTER LEADING THE photographer and his assistant to the staff quarters, the matron pauses in the midst of her bustling activity. She passes down a corridor that, to all appearances, is no different from any other. She stops by a door that is no different from all the other doors.

Why, then, does she grow damp about the armpits?

He is, after all, only an idiot.

But the matron, against her better judgment, has come to believe that there is something else, something yearning and human, something trapped inside that lumpy body, struggling to escape. She believes that she sees it in his eyes, the moment when he first awakes, and in his hands, when he defends himself from her washcloth. She felt it, perhaps, when he twisted away from her, and she pursued him, towel steaming; she felt it snuffling against her skirts, burrowing towards the warmth of her red hands. Something fierce and intelligent and alive.

The matron reports to the director: M. Jouy is in no condition to leave the hospital. He must remain under our care. The family will have to be informed.

foiled

THE CHEMIST READS THE LETTER, and then studies Mother, her bosom hefted dangerously atop his delicate display cases, with a little bit of dread. He takes two steps backwards.

Madame, he says, I hate to be the bearer of disappointing news.

I am not afraid, Mother says.

I regret to inform you that your request has been denied, the chemist says: M. Jouy cannot leave the hospital.

And the chemist is relieved to note that Mother appears unperturbed.

I have asked them politely, is all she says, before turning on her heels and leading her children in a majestic exit, each child clutching a caramel in one hand and an ingenious tin chicken in the other.

moustache

HAVING FINISHED OFF her bonbon, Beatrice raises her objections.

Madeleine belongs to us, she says. Why must we give her away?

Because, explains Mother, in good families, such as ours, it's best that girls of a certain age, and of certain experiences, be married.

But there are hundreds of nicer husbands, says Beatrice. What about that man who appeared at our door, the one with the moustache?

It is out of my hands, Mother says. Madeleine herself has chosen M. Jouy. In Nature's eyes, he is already her husband.

If that were true, Beatrice thinks, then he would be married to half the girls in our village.

Besides, Mother adds, he is agreeable, and undemanding. He will not complain about a wife who is often asleep.

Always asleep, says Beatrice.

He will not complain. Because how can he? When he himself is—

Lacking?

Yes, that's a fair way of putting it. To bring two people together, two incomplete people, is the right thing to do.

She was not always lacking, Beatrice thinks.

And do not forget, says Mother, what a help M. Jouy will be to have around the house. Remember how we used to pay him, in the springtime, to clean the shed? A son-in-law is what your father needs. One who is strong, with a healthy back, and who can keep him company.

Oh yes, says Beatrice, mechanically. It's the least we can do for Papa.

But you stay away from him, Mother warns.

Of course, Beatrice murmurs, lashes lowered.

inmate

MADELEINE LOOKS FOR M. Pujol. She is, however, too short. Even
hopping up and down, she still cannot see through the small, paned
windows at the top of every door, windows through which the
director can peer solicitously at the patient residing within. She
has worked her way down the corridor, and every window, it turns
out, has been constructed at the same impossible height.

Madeleine wishes to see the madmen and madwomen who live
inside the hospital. She expects that behind each door there exists
an amazing affliction: the Tigress, who paces her cell and feasts
upon raw livers; the Dromedary Boy, who fancies himself capable
of drinking a well dry; the Walrus Woman, who wept so profusely,
and at so little provocation, that her eyeteeth grew to the very
length and consistency of tusks. A man fluent in eleven languages,
yet unable to communicate with anyone. A girl who cannot seem
to stop sleeping, who rustles and stirs but never wakes.

The photographer, however, is six and a half inches taller than
Madeleine, a height from which he can peer through the windows,
only to discover the most ordinary of inmates. To visit this hospital,
he thinks, is to visit the catacombs and sewers of Paris; it is to stroll
down their broad avenues, admiring the symmetry of their arches.
Baron Hausmann has constructed, underground, a city nearly
identical to the one above: airy, harmonious, prosaic—a place that
invites slow perambulation, the opening of shops, the planning
of excursions. Touring through this subterranean city, one is struck
by the decorative arrangement of skulls, set into the walls like

Portuguese tiles, and the shininess of the piping through which the sewage rushes.

And here, in the hospital? The Walrus Woman is suffering from neurasthenia; the Man from Babel is afflicted by dementia praecox; the Tigress, a brain gone spongy from syphilis.

pose

THE DIRECTOR ATTACHES, by means of very small clamps, the
ends of six narrow wires to the fleshiest parts of a patient's face.
These wires connect the patient to a highly sensitive machine, the
newest of its kind, which is too large to appear in the photograph
itself. The machine looms darkly in the background; it takes up an
entire wall. Three serious men stand before it, adjusting its dials.
Or this is the impression that the director hopes to effect. The wires
do not, in fact, lead anywhere. They protrude crookedly from the
patient's head, and this, combined with the dullness of his eyes,
suggests a mutinous automaton, one who has tugged himself free
from the clockwork. While those that are wild-eyed, what they
resemble most are gorgons.

recognition

BENT OVER THE FIRE, Mother hatches a plan: small bodies creeping in the night, and then, at the hospital wall, each hoisted upon the shoulders of another. A stairway of children. The very highest step will be Claude: he raps on the window, awakens the slow-witted giant inside. Open the window! the boy urges. I have something for you!

A delicious lure, baked by Mother; a series of soft, mournful bird calls; a pony cart rolled out into position; an idiot falling through the darkness. When he lands, the cart wheels nearly break. The grain sacks exhale huge clouds of dust. The horse rears up, and then is quieted. The staircase dismantles itself. The bridegroom is abducted.

As Mother devises the retreat, a hand mirror appears before her. Beatrice is holding it; she has captured, again, something resembling a cow.

Do not worry, Beatrice says, Madeleine is still sleeping.

In the roundness of the mirror, Mother sees her own face captured. She sees how her eyes are shining, and her mouth clenched, in the great effort of bringing something forth, in the disfiguring strain of it. She barely understands the face as her own.

But I am not a monster, Mother says.

house of the sleeping beauties

TO MARRY, TO REAR HER CHILDREN, these things were on the surface good, Mother thinks. But to have had the long years in her power, to have controlled their lives, to have warped their natures even, these might be evil things.

Perhaps, beguiled by custom and order, one's sense of evil goes numb.

alphabet

IT IS TIME to begin.

This photograph shall be titled, Terror!

Terror? Adrien wonders, beneath his black hood.

You must make the subject appear terrified! says the director. Fear will be the first entry in our alphabet.

How am I to do that? Adrien asks, hidden behind his camera.

This is your science, not mine, says the director with respect. I will stand here, out of the way, and quietly watch you at work.

the photographer tries

WHEN THEY WERE CHILDREN, Adrien's brother owned a flock of racing pigeons. The pigeons lived in a loft atop the family's barn, and every night Adrien listened to the rub and flutter of their grey wings. Every day his brother trained them, and he watched, following his brother farther and farther away from home, across pastures, through villages, into places he had never been. Always at the moment he felt most thirsty and discouraged, his brother would lift his hands above his head and throw the pigeon into the sky. How loud the wings sounded! As loud as a thunderclap; as loud as the sound of his brother, whooping. It was the elation of this instant that made him walk such distances, in such silence. He wished one day to race pigeons of his own.

earthbound

BUT HIS BROTHER THOUGHT him better suited to keeping rabbits. While he loved all airborne things, Adrien was the kind who lived close to the ground, who liked to sit under tables, and press his cheek against moss.

His brother had dedicated each of his pigeons to a Roman emperor, a method of naming that struck Adrien as very sensible. So in his hutch, just as in his brother's pigeon loft, one could find a Tiberius, a Hadrian, a Marcus Aurelius, a Nero.

He might have been a good rabbit keeper, but he was forgetful, and this often resulted in their escape. He would forget to secure the latch, or if he took them out for exercise, he would become absorbed in some other small thing and forget to watch them. Once, his rabbits spent an afternoon in the front parlor, where they ate the fringe off an ornamental shawl, and scattered their pellets in discreet places about the room.

gift

DURING THIS TIME Adrien fell in love with the neighbor's daughter, and gave her the only gift he had, a rabbit. But she already had a pet, a brown and white spaniel, so instead she had a muff made, to keep her hands warm when she went ice-skating in the winter. He did not inform his brother of this exchange.

But he was afraid that his brother would notice something missing. Where's Augustus? he might ask, and then Adrien would have to tell him. For this reason he grew anxious in his brother's presence, starting when he entered a room, and jigging around the hutch, to distract him, whenever he drew near. When his brother asked him to display his rabbits at the fair, he refused.

His brother did a simple thing, then: he awoke Adrien in the night, led him to the hutch, and as they stood before it, in the starlight, watching the rabbits sleep, their sides softly heaving, he stamped his foot and clapped his hands. Just once, and sharply. It was an act so simple, so sudden and mysterious, that even after he had knelt down, unfastened the latch, and emerged with a rabbit, limp in his grasp, Adrien still did not understand what had happened.

Don't you see, his brother said, in exasperation: They are timid creatures. I scared this one to death.

terror

ADRIEN BURSTS FROM behind his camera. With his foot, he stomps. With his hands, he claps.

With sympathy, the patient smiles.

Perhaps, whispers the director, a different method is required.

The photographer is apologetic: If only you knew Félix, he says. If only he were here.

But he is in Paris, on the boulevard des Capucines, where he is draping a length of dark velvet about the divine Sarah Bernhardt, so that her shoulders will not appear too skinny.

Oh Félix, he sighs. Félix.

Disappearing beneath his hood, Adrien continues to mutter the name, and each time he does so, it is with a new expression: meditatively, at first, but then in surprise, as if he has encountered, there in the darkness, the very person he happened to be thinking of. Félix! It is an exclamation of sheer and startled delight, and the reunion a happy one, if somewhat reproachful. The name is spoken in a playful, scolding tone, and then, Félix, he says, more mildly this time, to indicate that all is forgiven. But in the midst of this cheerful exchange, a note of worry is introduced. Félix? he asks. Félix? he says, with increasing agitation. Perhaps the friendly meeting has taken a turn. Perhaps old resentments are awakened, the brother's brow darkening, the brother pulling himself up to his full height. Félix, he squeaks. Félix, no! he says, now fully alarmed. But maybe the brother is not coming closer. Quite possibly, he is walking away. Quite possibly, he has tired of the encounter, has an appointment to keep, and wishes to continue on. Over and over again the photographer cries, and it is impossible to tell if his despair is that of a person menacingly approached, or that of a person left behind.

Félix! he cries. Félix! Félix! Félix!

The photograph is a success. In it, the patient wears an expression of fear.

objects lost on journeys

MADELEINE'S HANDS make her useless. But she jostles the wagon, stoops over the canisters, and squints at the bulbs, in order to create the appearance of usefulness.

Have you found him? Adrien whispers.

Not yet, Madeleine says. I'm too short.

Adrien balances a glass plate between his hands, its surface etched with a terrified face, and says, I am beginning to worry.

Have you ever, he wonders, begun a journey with a suitcase, and guarded that suitcase closely, keeping it beneath your bed at night, and watching over it at the station like a mother? Then the suitcase is lost, but you are consoled, because a lady passenger has given you a pair of eyeglasses with green-tinted lenses, and you guard them on your journey with all the care that you once bestowed upon your suitcase. Then the eyeglasses are shattered, but you hardly notice, you have become so attached to the first edition you found in a moldering bookshop. Then the first edition tumbles over the railing of the ferry, the ferry carrying you from one end of the lake to the other, and when you land, and see the pretty town on the side of the mountain, you remember: on a stiff card, tucked into the lining of your suitcase, there is written the address where you are expected.

Are you worried, Madeleine asks, that we will never find him?

I am worried, Adrien says, that I will leave the hospital, that I will travel for many days, and only upon wandering into a market and finding a stall selling figs, or meeting the eyes of a young prostitute, or stumbling over a mangy dog run out into the street, only then will I realize what I have forgotten to bring with me: M. Pujol.

usury

WHAT MADELEINE THINKS IS: Oh yes. I know what you mean exactly. Like the words: Orchard, swallow—but she cannot finish, because even to think her words again is to use them, to wear down the coins through repeated touching until they are of no value at all. So instead she says, stoutly: Do not worry. I will find him. And then we will all escape.

coupling

MADELEINE, IN SECRET, wonders what will happen after the
rescue takes place. There is the problem of numbers. The girl,
the photographer, the flatulent man: three of them panting on the
grass, with earth clumped in their eyebrows (escape by tunnel), or
welts rising on their wrists (escape by rope). Or perhaps they are
altogether untouched, having cooked a sticky and soporific pudding
which the matron, unknowing, served the director with his lunch.
Three people lie sprawled on the grass, chests hurting, the hospital
far behind them.

Will the flatulent man rise up on his elbows, seeing Madeleine
as if for the first time, noticing how well she looks, how bravely and
wisely she carries herself, how her complexion has brightened and
her figure filled out, how she has, in short, grown into a beautiful
woman? (Why did I not see it before? he wonders. Right beneath
my nose! he marvels.) Or will he roll onto his side, and find himself
gazing at a dreamy young man, of a gentle and accommodating
temperament, with whom he might retire to a fishing village on the
edge of a warm sea and develop a lasting friendship? (There will be
wine in the afternoons, he thinks; there will be a basket lowered and
raised from our window.) Will he rise up on his elbows, or will he
roll onto his side? It is impossible to predict.

If only a fourth should appear! The plucky kitchen boy, who
aided the escape. The cynical magistrate, heart softened by the
nobility of their cause. The long-lost fiancée, believed captured by
pirates, who has disguised herself as a foreign prince and earned a

174

university degree. The resourceful milkmaid; the soldier; the poet, disaffected with his art. Anyone would do. Even the matron, the director, the Dromedary Boy. All are loveable, once one learns how.

Because a certain symmetry is required. If not everyone is accounted for, the plot seems less bold, the escape less like an escape. What had once seemed a story is revealed as nothing more than a series of miscalculations, muddles, trap doors, false alarms.

new entry

BUT THERE IS NO NEED to continue searching for the flatulent man. He is delivered to them. Or to Adrien, at least, on a temporary basis: the subject for a study of Embarrassment.

M. Pujol's face, upon seeing the photographer, causes the director to reconsider. He is Stupefaction, the director cries, personified!

Adrien ducks behind his machinery. He, too, is taken by surprise. For here at the hospital, where hygiene is so furiously pursued, the matron has forbidden moustaches, especially those that require waxing, and M. Pujol's face, destitute of moustache, is hardly recognizable as his face at all. It would have been preferable if he had lost an eye. Also his body: it does not seem the same. Underneath the white smock that all the patients must wear, M. Pujol appears to be less perfectly slim, less gentlemanlike, and though Adrien has seen him a hundred times without clothes, the thought of it now horrifies him, faintly.

For this reason the photographer remains hidden beneath his black hood, even after the director has left them alone. He is afraid that if he were to emerge, his own face would be legible, a new entry for the alphabet. Under D, for Deadened Affection? No, that is not it, exactly. The sight of M. Pujol still provokes him. He is dismayed to feel something twitching, like the snout of a little dog rooting in the leaves. He snaps it backwards on its leash; his nose wrinkles at what it has found.

Perhaps, if M. Pujol were behind the camera and he in front of it, the photograph would be titled Repulsion.

pardon

THE WIDOW? She is well?
    We have come to rescue you.
    And the others in our company?
    But we haven't figured out a plan.
    So you are no longer taking art photographs?
    The girl and I. We came here.
    You have chosen, instead, the scientific. As I did!
    It will not be easy.
    Though I think I might be a disappointment to the director.
    She loves you.
    Apparently little can be learned without opening me up.
    I am just helping her.
    Could you say that again? Your voice. It is muffled.

what if

THE PONY CART, never known for its reliability, seems now in danger of collapsing altogether. It is unaccustomed to the weight of M. Jouy, who sits placidly at its edge, his feet dragging along the dim road and raising dust. To keep the cart from upsetting, all the brothers and sisters have scrambled to the front. They disagree over who will wield the switch. Their teeth rattle in their heads. But this cannot stop them from singing.

We are the most cunning family in the world! Claude shouts to the moon.

Jean-Luc, who has strained his back, is not as convinced of this.

Next we should kidnap the prime minister and demand ransom, says Lucie.

No! cries Mimi. He dislikes children, and will make an unpleasant prisoner. I say we should take the princess, who will do everything as we tell her.

Oh, it is easiest for the little ones! Jean-Luc moans.

To Claude's disappointment, M. Jouy has not joined them in their singing. He has not spoken, in fact, since his abduction, nor made any sound at all.

It is because his mouth is full, says Mimi.

Lucie makes a note of this: He has been taught good manners, even though he is an idiot.

What if we take away his cookie? Claude suggests.

But they shy away from the idea, these fierce-hearted children. It touches them strangely to see M. Jouy eating, the slow grinding movement of his terrible jaws, heavy as death. But he takes the tiniest of bites! It is like waking up the miller, setting those huge stones into motion, for only a half cup of meal. But this is clever, thinks Lucie. To make the cookie last.

I know, says Jean-Luc, forgetting for a moment the pain in his back: What if we were to flick him, lightly, with the switch?

hold me

MADELEINE STIRS IN HER SLEEP. She opens her eyes to see the photographer, his face close to hers. In this half light, she is not afraid to reach up and touch it with her ruined hand.

What is happening? From the corridor outside she hears the ringing of a hundred little bells, bells meant for summoning the director to his dinner or announcing the arrival of a visitor, but now their small polite voices are raised all at once, in alarm. The long hallway hisses with the sound of slippered feet.

A patient was kidnapped, the photographer whispers. And knowing that the matron is thus occupied, he lifts up the covers on Madeleine's cot and climbs in beside her.

They lie close together for a long time. The girl breathes so heavily he thinks she is asleep.

But then she says, clearly, So it can be done.

He moves her hand. He places it carefully. She is talking about escape.

delivery

JEAN-LUC EXPECTS to receive some credit for the cruelty of his suggestion. But Beatrice only laughs at him. A switch! How childish. Her laugh reveals every way in which his thinking is tedious and quaint. Jean-Luc returns sadly to nursing the strain in his back. She acts as if she is the oldest of them all now.

She turns and looks at the other children, daringly.

You want to hear him talk? she asks.

Not one of them says yes. But she doesn't need them to. The horse lets out a little groan when she pulls on the reins, a warning he might not get started back up again. She's heard it before; she drops down onto the road, marches to the rear of the cart. On her face is the sly, important expression that the postman wears while making deliveries. She pretends as if she doesn't notice how hungrily her brothers and sisters are watching her. And then, with the same neatness of movement, the same absence of imagination with which she straightens the tablecloth, wrings the laundry, beats the carpets, dresses the children, heeds her mother's every command, she lifts the edge of M. Jouy's smock so that she can unbutton the opening to his breeches.

The children, too, let out a little groan. This is a constant source of wonder to them, that Beatrice should appear docile while being so profoundly disobedient.

dominoes

MADELEINE'S VOICE beside him is incredulous.

You found him?

In his hurry, he forgot to mention it. It was not what he was thinking of, as he slid into the cot.

Why didn't you come get me?

She sits up. She grabs his shoulder with her sticky hand and shakes him.

I was playing dominoes in the pantry, she says. As I always do.

Her head wags back and forth in bewilderment.

In the pantry, she says. Just down the stairs.

He knew that; he did. From the embittered cook, she had already won twenty-two cigarettes, which she kept in a biscuit tin at the bottom of his wagon and often asked him to recount.

I don't understand, she says slowly, while poking him. We had a conspiracy.

When she jabs her hand at his chest, it feels searching, not spiteful. She brings her face down to look at him, and he thinks for a moment that she is going to press her ear against his heart and listen.

Then she subsides, without warning. The sticky hand is withdrawn. She inhales sharply, in discovery.

Oh! she breathes. The two of you—

He wishes that she would poke him again, or shake him. That she would not take away her hand.

But full of understanding, she whispers to him:

You wanted to be alone.

unmanned

WE CANNOT LEAVE HIM ALONE! the children wail, clutching onto the sides of the pony cart. They take turns staring miserably after the half-wit and directing poisonous glances at their sister. Horrible girl! It was not his fault, they are certain of it: all the blame they reserve for heartless, bungling Beatrice.

Mother will thank me, she says as she applies, with cruel precision, the switch. The cart lurches forward: He's no good as a husband.

But he had nice manners! they protest.

Who needs manners? snaps Beatrice. His cock stopped working at the hospital!

That seems an unfair way of putting it.

You just didn't know how to work it properly, declares Mimi, the youngest and also the most foolhardy. In her eyes there is a defiant look, always, even when she is about to fall asleep. *I despise sleep!* her shining eyes declare as the lids droop ever more heavily downwards.

Drunk with her own courage she continues, unwisely: I don't think you pulled it hard enough.

For there he is, standing in the ditch, in the moonlight, with his smooth face and his noble body, not looking broken or imperfect at all.

I don't think you knew what you were doing, Mimi persists.

Beatrice swivels in her seat and gazes down at her siblings, huddled in the back of the pony cart, wincing in expectation.

183

The load is so much lighter now, she says, without fury. And then: We can go even faster if we let off one more.

This observation having been offered, the brothers and sisters keep their complaints to themselves. Instead, they stare behind them at the idiot, who, with every flick of the switch, grows smaller and more indistinct, though they are certain they can still make out, even from here, the slow hypnotic churning of his jaws.

a puzzle

YOU WANTED to be alone, Madeleine says.

Rather than answer, the photographer embraces her, and for one or two minutes it feels fairly wonderful. Her nose sunk in his shirt, his arms around her; her breathing, without permission, falling in step with his own. Ahhhhhhh, she thinks, words leaving her. Ahhhhhhhh. There is only weight, warmth, covers, breath. Far down below, their feet touch.

But after one or two minutes have passed, the embrace becomes intolerable. Madeleine believes that she will die, that if she can't escape the arm, or kick her feet out from beneath the covers, she will surely, quickly, quietly die. She feels the panic of the dying: a swarming on her skin; a series of soft explosions coming closer; the difficulty of finding her next breath.

So she twitches, lets out a sigh; she acts as if sleep has come to take her. He relinquishes her then, he delivers her up. The parting is easier this way. And he curls over on his other side, tucking his hands beneath his cheek.

She is not sleepy in the least. She wants only the coldest part of the bed and slides to the far edge in search of it. But as soon as she arrives, she misses him. She would like to eat him up, if possible, or else be eaten up herself. If she were to kiss every part of his body, it would not be enough. She could gnaw at the back of his neck, suck on his fingers, cup his nose in the warm cave of her mouth and it would not suffice. To smother herself in his nice-smelling shirt, allowing his weight to extinguish her last breath, would still leave her wanting him. And he is not even the one she loves.

She cannot tell which is more strange: enjoying his closeness, or thinking she might die, or suffering this sad bout of appetite.

denied

TOMORROW, THEN? Madeleine asks.

And with a sick heart she imagines the three of them panting on the grass, the hospital a glittering red shard in the distance; M. Pujol rolling on his side to gaze at the photographer and the photographer, beneath his gaze, beginning to smile (there will be wine in the afternoons, a basket lowered and raised from the window); and the act thus coming to its end, the night descending swiftly like a curtain—but then, there in the dusk, is the pop of a tin being opened. The shadow beside M. Pujol releases into the air an unmistakable smell, a shadow with small shoulders and two great mittens for hands. It leans closer, becoming Madeleine. She is offering him a selection of twenty-two cigarettes. They tempt him; he chooses one, and as he draws up onto his elbows to accept her burning match, he is astonished to observe how well she looks, how her complexion has brightened and her features softened, how resourceful she is, and generous, how irresistible the scent of her cigarettes—

Madeleine turns to the wall. She has got it all wrong. Open a tin? Light a match? She vows to return her winnings to the cook. The cot creaks beneath her, the photographer sighing. He is not answering her questions.

Again she asks, Tomorrow?

Adrien reaches for her hands but cannot find them.

Tomorrow? she asks, back curved away, withholding everything.

He does not want to come with us, Adrien admits at last.

song

THEY WILL COME SOON, Mother thinks, and puts flowers in a jar, tugging them up from between the floorboards. Her blessed children, and a bridegroom! She sings to herself in a low, gay voice, one she hasn't used in a long time, perhaps since her discovery of the mole on her husband's side, blooming just beneath his ribs like a small patch of lichen. All this time, and yet something new! How wonderful that his body, so well known to her, should still be capable of surprises. Such are the gifts of marriage.

I will count them for you, she sings to her daughter, her hair drying on the pillowcase. And upon finding herself unable to do so, she croons, They are without number.

madeleine reasons

WHY WON'T M. PUJOL leave the hospital?

Because he is without hope.

How did he lose hope?

By accepting that he will never have what he wants.

What does M. Pujol want?

He wants to perform as he once did, in a theatre, wearing a tailcoat.

And why can he no longer perform?

Because audiences care little for authenticity or artistry.

No, truly, why can't he?

Because he requires an audience that is quaint, small-minded, suspicious, excitable, easily made red in the face. And such an audience can no longer be found in Paris. Or Toulouse. Or the Bois. Or many other places in the world.

the photographer dreams

HAVING SORTED OUT THE FACTS, Madeleine whispers to the photographer: I plan to build him a stage. In my town, where they will love him. Then you can show him the poster, with his name on it, and he will be persuaded to come.

A stage? repeats the photographer, half-asleep. He finds her hand; he holds it up to the dim windows.

You? Build a stage?

He presses his mouth against her hand and kisses it.

Yes, Madeleine says, a real stage, inside a grand theatre, large enough to fit all the people in my town. There will be little footlights, and a velvet curtain, a printed program, and—

A poster. His name. A picture: a man delicately parting the tails of his coat. And letters, she is saying, tall red ones, as Adrien slips off to have a dream about his brother. In his dream he moves more freely than usual, leaping over things, yelping, swinging his arms high above his head. If he runs, he is able to keep up with Félix quite easily. And off they go crashing into a pond, where they slap the water's surface with their outstretched arms, as though they had grown the heavy wings of a swan.

When he wakes, light pouring through the windows, he finds himself spread selfishly across the cot, sheets bunched at his feet, and she, with her sticky hands, already gone.

dowry

FROM THE CURVE in the road, the children can already see their mother, doubled over and heaving, exiting from the doorway backside first. She moves with the narrow, shuffling steps of a person towing a much larger and more lifeless body. Why hasn't she called Father for help? And all at once they turn pale, for having arrived unannounced they have done it at last: caught Mother in the midst of her private activities.

It's not Madeleine? Lucie asks, in a quavering voice.

No, says Jean-Luc, who is taller and proportionately less dramatic: It is only Mother's chest.

Only! The girls rise up on their toes, straining to see for themselves. The chest is forbidden to them, never opened, frequently polished, smelling faintly of candles when they press their furtive noses against its seams. Inside, they are told, they will one day find their mother's most beautiful things. And so Beatrice imagines a spill of silk underclothes, light as froth, and Mimi, who believes her mother's tastes to be in perfect accord with her own, pictures the glistening brown eyes of the tame monkey she longs for, while Lucie imagines a mirror, brimming at the edge of the chest like a pool: when the lid is finally raised, she will gaze down at its clear surface, seeing her own face, and those of her sisters.

No one imagines a veil.

A veil! Beatrice gasps, as Mother lifts it from the open chest, its sheer white length floating out from her fingers. A thousand tiny stitches hang aloft in the morning air. They have heard of this veil;

191

how many times has their mother described the putting on of it, the splendid wearing of it, the lifting of it to disclose her husband's gentle, nervous face, peering down at her? How lightly it must have rested upon her hair! Up, up it rises, curling like smoke, until at last it dissolves into a great cloud of goosedown, peculiar goosedown, which, rather than slowly tumbling to the ground, darts off merrily in all directions, the thousand stitches revealing themselves as moths.

unveiled

OH NO, MURMURS BEATRICE, who has watched her mother greet the bad news of ripped sheets, a sick cow, burnt bread, curdled milk, with an alarming degree of outrage. And now this, a true tragedy—perhaps they had better turn around and come home tomorrow.

But Mimi, the youngest and most foolhardy, has already leapt down from the cart and begun running towards the house. As her feet fly beneath her, as her breathing quickens and the long grasses wave her on from the side of the road, she thinks, with each shuddering burst of her heart, That is my mother. There she is.

Maman! she cries, coming closer, and the familiar figure turning towards her, arms spread. Maman! she shouts, for she is running to meet her mother, with her thick waist and her deep skirts and her dark, intoxicating smell. So pretty! is what she sobs before sinking far into her mother's folds. Then, surfacing only long enough to say it, her face swollen, her eyes swimming with love: You must have looked so pretty.

For this is a revelation to Mimi, that Mother for her wedding wore moths in her hair, a revelation that casts her in an entirely new light.

reel

MADELEINE IS CARRIED HOME in the company of bees. Before sunrise, she walks away from the hospital at Maréville, until in the darkness she comes upon a wagon, lit by a dying lantern and driven by a drowsing boy, whose head lists far to one side as he is pulled helplessly back into sleep. It is with hardly any effort at all that she breaks into a little run and scrambles up among the beehives on their way to Saturday market, the boy not even turning around or murmuring in protest.

She leans against the hives and dangles her feet over the edge of the dray, watching the road unfurl in her wake. To move backwards in this way through the landscape that she left long ago—it makes her feel like a kite being reeled in from the sky. Passing beneath her are dusky fields, linden trees, a scattering of stony houses. The sleeping boy pulls her forever back, past the cupola atop the mayor's new house, past the slate roofs and the barely smoking chimneys, past the sprigged curtains hanging in upper windows, the painted doorways, the homely fences with their latched gates, past the pigsties and the henhouses, past the little low bench where her mother sometimes liked to catch her breath. And though Madeleine knows that her long spell of weightlessness has finally come to its end—the tug of the string, the smell of damp earth—she feels, contrary to all expectations, her heart begin to lift.

log

MME. COCHON TOUCHES DOWN upon the chemist's shop. Here, with a light wind blowing and the sun still caught behind the church, she pulls her diary from between her breasts. She presses the tip of a pencil to her tongue.

In the left-hand column, she notes:

At dawn, ate a plum. Bitter. Spit it out. Saw wagon on road to Saint Nicholas. Beehives in back. Madeleine slid out. Pangs of indigestion. Watched her walk into woods. Dress needing a good scrub.

For now, the right-hand column remains empty. Mme. Cochon is not her regular self today.

On the left, she continues:

Mid-morning, took some tea. Appetite returning. Clouds dispersed. Wanting jar of pear jam. No chance to ask. Children arrived with cart. Beauty in back.

It is the sight of this stranger, sitting in the pony cart, that prompts Mme. Cochon to write her first full sentence of the day.

She must drink vinegar to keep herself so slim.

visitor

BEATRICE DOES NOT RISK making the introduction immediately, as Mother hails her triumphant children parading through the yard, the moth-eaten veil all but forgotten, the chest abandoned by the doorstep, but of her own accord the stray woman dismounts from the cart and inches towards the gate, where she waits to be noticed, invited in.

Mother straightens, plucking Mimi's arms from about her waist: Who is that?

There are gypsies wandering about, and thieves, and she has also heard many chilling accounts of kidnappers. As for this woman, is that a trick of the light, that makes the shape of her head seem familiar? It is unnerving, the way she gazes so wistfully at the house, the yard, the swarm of clamoring children. Yes, she is well-dressed, but her hand crawls up and down the length of her pale neck like a spider.

The sight of this stranger prompts Mother to ask: Where is M. Jouy?

Oh Mother, Beatrice exclaims, what a story we have to tell you!

And as if on cue the other children stop where they are and drop down onto their bottoms, elbows on knees, chins in hands, rapt faces turned towards their sister. Mother, her suspicions aroused, her eyebrows raised, remains standing. It is difficult to tell whom she regards with greater misgiving: her gesticulating daughter, grown so tall now, or the vagrant woman hovering outside her gate.

beatrice says

ON THE ROAD WE FOUND a woman, covered in blood. As she walked, she left behind her a trail of red drops, falling from her hair and her sleeves and the tip of her chin. But she was so beautiful, so much more beautiful than we could ever imagine, we stopped the horse and asked her to come with us.

We wanted to know, Why are you covered in blood?

She told us, It is the blood of my husband. I returned to him because I had grown lonely for the sight of my face, and for the sound of my voice.

We asked her, How lonely?

And she told us, So lonely that I heard it in the branches of trees, in cart wheels and doorknobs, in the moans of a flatulent man, in all kinds of wind. And though I scraped on my body and ordered it to speak, the sounds I made were strange to me.

And so I went home to my husband, and as soon as I stepped into his gardens, I heard him playing. I heard the sound of my own voice, carrying to me from an upstairs window. But when I entered his house, the viol fell silent, and all that I found, sitting down to his supper, was my enormous husband—

And then she killed him! Claude cries as he slices an invisible sword through the air.

hello

CLAUDE IS BANISHED to the orchard, to say hello to his father.

I'm home! the boy cries.

So you are, observes his father, arms high above his head, hands lost in the mottled ceiling of the leaves.

When his hands emerge, holding apples, he offers one to Claude.

And your trip, Father asks, it was pleasant?

Claude nods, mouth occupied.

And the horse did not complain?

Claude shrugs his shoulders.

Tell me, Father says, where is it that you went?

As Claude struggles to swallow, Father apologizes.

Your mother—she has a business, she's thinking all the time—and with her mind so full, she sometimes forgets to tell me.

Claude takes another bite, so he doesn't have to answer.

underworld

AS I WAS SAYING, Beatrice perseveres.

My husband seemed not at all surprised to see me, perhaps because he had grown so used to looking at my face. Where is Griselda? I demanded, and he merely shrugged, intent upon helping himself to a great quivering pudding.

In the scrapheap, I suppose, is all my husband said. And then he considered: Or maybe burned as firewood last winter, when it grew so very cold.

I watched as he carved off the glistening leg of a goose.

On further thought, said my husband, it is most likely at the orphanage, because in my old age I have cultivated the habit of charity. Did you know that they are musical, orphans?

I knew only that my husband was lying. For hadn't I heard her raise her lament, heard her sobbing to me from across the gardens? And who better than I to recognize the sound of my own voice?

See for yourself, my husband told me. And off I ran into the dark passageways of his house, a black labyrinth of chambers and corridors that had remained, even when I lived among them, impenetrable to me. But now I moved through them with a strange clarity of purpose, as though a little lamp were burning before me, and the doors I remembered as locked now fell open beneath my fingertips. Room after room of his mother's shrouded furniture; and my old bedchamber sheathed in white; and his libraries, the books rising untouched from floor to ceiling; and his practice room, spare as a cell, with sheets of music still spread on the stand—

Don't bother with all the rooms, says Lucie impatiently. Tell about the *girls*.

sylph

AWAY FROM HIS FATHER Claude drifts, kicking at the apples on the ground, his neck bent, his gaze fastened downward. When at last he looks up, he thinks he sees, flickering at the edge of the orchard, a girl. But she moves so quickly through the crooked trees—is it two girls? Or three?

viscera

IN THE FARTHEST CORNER of the smallest practice room, a room
so small and nearly forgotten that even the curls of rosin on the
floor had gathered dust, there was a little door, like one covering
a cupboard, and behind this door is where my husband kept his
failed compositions. If ever another human eye should see these, he
once confessed, I would die of humiliation. And when he said this
to me, I took pity on him, for indeed his eyes watered and his lip
trembled, and for an instant it did seem possible that his huge
distended heart might collapse upon itself in shame. So though
I crept repeatedly into his practice rooms, I never once disturbed
that little cupboard door.

But upon my return, I noted that the cupboard door stood
ajar, as if opened from the inside by a very faint draft. And I was
overpowered. By my own curiosity. My hands shook, my breath
faltered, and the door opened to reveal not sagging shelves but a
passageway ablaze with light. And rooms, yes, more rooms (had
Lucie been present she would have received a deadly look, but
Lucie, too, has been sent away), unlike those I had ever seen inside
my husband's house. Rooms without windows, but lit from within
by such brilliant colors, the strange color and light that emanates
from expensive things: walrus tusks, snuff bottles, paintings so black
that nothing could be discerned but a cheekbone or an eye,
tapestries of rape, swords with sharkskin hilts, tiny jeweled boxes
whose interiors rattled. I wanted to touch everything at once.

When I reached out to feel the tapestry, I saw her: long neck, seven strings, melancholy face. She was turned halfway to the wall, as if in embarrassment, propped between a footstool and a glass case displaying postage stamps. And selfishly I felt only joy: it was not Griselda, trapped in this airless place. But who was she, with her weak jaw and her melancholy expression?

echo

WANDERING THROUGH THE ORCHARD, Claude wonders, Who
was she?

appetite

WHY DID SHE WATCH so sadly out of the corner of her eye? Following her gaze, I understood, for there was another, stripped of her body, who, together with a covey of umbrella handles, was peering timidly from a severed elephant's foot. Prompted by their poor pleading faces, I went from room to room, finding more: those with gaping, half-finished bodies; those with their own strings twisted about their necks like a noose; also the decapitated, their heads turned to paperweights. It took no effort to imagine what had happened in these brilliant rooms. What hunger, on his part. What extreme terror on theirs. And my whole self trembled then: in pity for what they had suffered, perhaps, or in relief that my own face was not among them, but in truth I think I shook only with the cool exhilaration of being right.

For I had known all along. I had known when I sat down to dinner with my husband, when I spent the afternoon by a window reading a book, or drifted down the dark corridors of his house, feeling my way to his bed. I had known of their terror, that they languished on the other side of the wall, yet I had moved through the corridors thinking only of my dinner, my book, his bed, my lovely face. I had known of them in their bright hidden rooms, and at last I was here, shaking in triumph, sick with my own acuity, sick with the pleasure of being right.

It was with this sickness and elation that I sought out my husband, knowing now where I would find Griselda. For wasn't the appetite of my husband as cruel as the wolf's, as great as the whale's? In one despairing gulp, he had swallowed her.

saboteur

THE STORY IS TOO LONG, Mother interrupts. All those dinners, those corridors. And where is M. Jouy? I fixed him something special to eat.

Beatrice's face, her hands, collapse: But I haven't finished.

I already know what is going to happen, Mother says. Claude told us at the beginning.

Do you understand how difficult it is, to slice someone open with a carving knife? His intestines—his liver—his marbled heart—

This is why I use the butcher, Mother says. Where is M. Jouy?

Don't you wonder if she found Griselda?

I made him sausages!

Mother and Beatrice stare at each other, white-lipped, ill-matched in their obduracy.

The daughter relents. But this is the best part, she says mournfully.

And seeking encouragement, she finds none, for Mimi has been exiled for coughing, Jean-Luc for looking bored, and the only audience remaining is her unimaginative mother.

Blood everywhere, she murmurs as her audience stalks off, in search of an idiot.

And when the curdling cries rise up from the shed, when the cart is found empty and the bridegroom missing, Beatrice watches in regret the woman backing from their gate, whose tragic story, it must be admitted, she somewhat mismanaged. If only her brothers and sisters were not capable of such sabotage! She had gotten rid of a useless thing, put a beautiful thing in its place, and yet they were, all of them, intent upon finding fault and thwarting her.

Her sense of injustice is so strong that she stamps her foot against the ground and then, with the other foot, kicks her mother's precious, pointless chest.

instinct

AT THE FAR EDGE of the orchard Madeleine freezes. What is that sound? A howl of fury, a long barking cry. Like a lick of flame it flares up from the shed in the distance, threatening to burn down the whole world around it. My home is not my home, it cries, my children not my children; all that I thought was mine is alien to me. Like the smell of smoke it snakes its way to where Madeleine stands frozen; it sets the apple leaves trembling, lifts the birds from where they feast upon the orchard floor. And Madeleine herself, like a wild forgotten thing, begins to stir: her ears prick, her eyes water, and bringing them up to her mouth, she cups her misshapen hands and lets out her own long howl of sympathy.

stirring

MADELEINE STIRS IN HER SLEEP. Her eyelids flutter open.
What is that sound? From deep inside her dream she heard it: a
wail. An inconsolable cry. It is a voice she thinks she recognizes,
and sliding out from beneath her covers, she steals off into the
orchard to meet it.

beating

THE BROTHERS AND SISTERS cannot sleep, with Mother outside in the yard and still angry. *Thunk, thunk* beneath their window, quickening like a heartbeat, while the children lie stiff in their beds, fearing that, in her excitement, Mother might send fruit hurtling through the glass. Pitched with enough force, an underripe pear could leave a small person unconscious.

Claude thinks it would be wise to slip off and make himself scarce. Down the ladder he goes, into the larder, filling his pockets, feeling the floor grave-cold beneath his feet, dreaming of what he will find inside the barn. Not a proper cowshed like their own, with a pony cart and six cows and a collection of deadly tools, hung in descending order against the wall; but a forgotten barn, a skeletal barn, where he is not allowed to go. That is where the half-wit once slept, the moon coming through the rafters and casting him in white stripes. But tonight, the boy dreams, the barn is thick with an apple smell and small rustling noises, the titters and sighs of girls settling into sleep: three of them, he now believes, most definitely three. Three girls flickering through the branches, roosting inside the forbidden barn and he, Claude, the only one to know of them.

They must be hungry, he thinks as he touches his swollen pockets. And then his heart stops; for that other heartbeat, thick and wet, has stopped too. I'm through, he thinks, his hands crammed in his pockets. But then it resumes—*thunk, thunk*—and the boy steps out into the night.

lunar

SEEING THE MOON through the rafters, Madeleine remembers other moons, the same moon: a grey coin dim in the window above her siblings' bed; a golden balloon snagging upon the spires of a city; the sliver that curved away from her as she tumbled off a caravan's slick roof.

What moon, she wonders, is looking down upon the hospital at Maréville? Why, a moon as round and mild as her own face, with eyes set far apart, the forehead high. Shedding light as she once shed droplets of water, her face emerging from the basin. A half-smile, a pox scar, a pair of eyebrows pale as wheat. Madeleine is moon-faced, her mother would say as she handed her the towel, and from that fact deduce a hundred other things, among them a guileless nature, a love of cream. But did she know this luminous face would wake inmates in the asylum, make women bleed, open night-blooming vines, pull everything irresistibly towards it?

Inside the hospital at Maréville, the photographer turns the flatulent man to the window and says, Look.

anatomy

BUT M. PUJOL CANNOT LOOK; he is too distracted to look. For
the photographer has stepped out from behind his equipment. He
has placed his hands on the flatulent man's shoulders; he has kept
his hands on the trembling shoulders; he has turned him to the
window under the guidance of his hands.

M. Pujol is now familiar with names, due to the great black
anatomy book the director has been kind enough to share with
him. So when the hands slide downward from his shoulders,
M. Pujol's first thought is, My scapulae. These are the two
triangular blades. Thinking such thoughts, recalling such names,
might possibly prevent him from trembling. As the hands travel,
so do his thoughts: There are my vertebrae, he thinks, as the hands
drift ever downwards to the sacrum. The sacrum, the sacred bone,
the spot where his fluttering soul resides. On this point, and on
many others, M. Pujol is in accordance with the Greeks. Not the
heart, nor the head, but the very bottom of the spine: this is where
the photographer will find him. Upon reaching the crossroads—my
sacroiliac, he gasps—the two hands part company, one turning to
the west, the other to the east, and on its own each traces the crest
of his hipbones.

As the hands advance along the ilium, he feels a pair of lips
upon his neck. Lips, plural; neck, the nape of—but already the
name for lips, the name for neck, have escaped him.

under the gaze of the moon

M. PUJOL CLOSES HIS EYES; relinquishes names; makes his surrender. It is as she wishes.

waxing

AS CLAUDE STUMBLES through the orchard, his expectations take on form, enormous size. They will have soft fingers. And gleaming hair. Their nipples will be tiny and wild as strawberries. In an interesting coincidence, Claude found a patch of berries last summer behind this same barn. He kept them to himself. He made visits when no one was looking. And remembering how shyly the berries appeared when he lifted up the canopy of their leaves, Claude pictures the girls' sleepy faces, their looks of surprise. How delighted they will be to see him.

The barn is bathed in moonlight. Claude presses his face to a crack in the door. He wants simply a glance, an unhurried glance, before he comes in and startles them. Maybe he will catch them as they are brushing each other's hair, or softly embracing, or kissing good night. Countless entrancing scenes could await him, but when he presses his face to the crack in the door, the sight he finds disturbs him.

There is only one girl, not three. She is lying on the floor of the barn. She is small, and wearing a filthy party dress, and appears to have been dropped down from another world. But not in the pleasant way he was expecting. Her body lies rigid except for her hand, which is tucked between her legs and moving desperately. Though her face is turned away from him, Claude believes that its expression must be of suffering. Look at the violence she does to herself! She is in thrall to that furious hand. He forgets the nipples, the shining hair: his thought is to save her, to knock down the

214

rotting door and make it stop. But there is something in the way she stiffens that tells him such a rescue would be unwelcome. That annihilation is in fact her purpose. That she wants nothing more than this hand, this moon, this forgotten barn, conspiring to release her, to rub her out.

Claude knows where he's not wanted. He has several sisters, an older brother; he is familiar with the feeling. His hopes and gifts hang heavily on him. As he backs away from the awful barn, he empties his swollen pockets of their sausages.

waning

THE PHOTOGRAPHER LIFTS his mouth from the neck of the flatulent man, and the moon turns away from them, diminished. Her hand drops to her side.

buried

IN THE MORNING Madeleine finds, lying on the ground, three sausages. Not wrapped in brown paper, or set on a plate, but poking out from the spiky grass that grows alongside the barn, as if the earth itself had offered them up overnight. They are good-looking, and smell quite deliciously of garlic. Madeleine knows that some further investigation is probably required, but she is hungry, and blessed, according to her mother, with the stomach of an ox.

All that's needed is a little knife, some radishes. Without thinking, she pushes her hands into the soil and feels about. It is not a wishful or improbable thing to do. Her father once found a coin. Another man, a pale blue bottle. Why not a knife? Or, for that matter, a copper tub, a flask of wine, a rolling pin? A king's kitchen could be waiting down below, all flashing utensils and giant vats, the cook with her cleaver raised, the scullery maid weeping, their poor old mouths filled with dirt.

What's that rumbling then, but the heave-ho of the earth sending up its lost city, its thoroughfares and byways, its traffic jams and slop jars, broken hearts, stillborns, waiting rooms, concert halls, card games and night terrors, its quick-witted children, its constables and beggars, usurers, pilots, its laughing women, its libraries, its collection of familiar, half-forgotten lives? It could be the sound of a girl's empty stomach. Madeleine sinks her ear into the ground and listens: yes, there it is, beneath the tumult of her blood, a tapping. From the city down below, a sound; a sign. The knife against the chopping board? The cook putting down her cleaver? Tap-tap, it says, then hesitates. A blind man's cane. A teacher's ruler. Tap-tap, it says again and all at once she knows: stacked heel. Worn floorboards. A hesitation in the step, a stutter. Should he draw the sword here? Or wait until the final line? Should he pause before the 'O'? The tap-tapping of an actor, pacing. He turns his eyes to the soil-black heavens and sighs; she hears now only the anguish of the 'O!' And in this very place, she knows, there was once a stage.

surprise

MADELEINE'S HANDS dig deeper, searching for a tin of pastilles, a pair of opera glasses, the buckle from a stagehand's belt. It would be lovely to find something useful, something with which she could begin: like a nail. The earth feels cool as she shovels through it. But then, there in the soil, is something warm. And twisting. It wriggles against her with curiosity, or possibly affection. It is not, she hopes, a worm. She would not like to have such a humble thing attached to her. For when she moves her hands through the dirt, it follows.

If she pulls herself rudely enough from the ground, if she stamps her feet and flaps her arms and trembles all over like a tambourine, then perhaps the worm will think better of the arrangement, and leave her alone.

Madeleine shakes so hard that the sky turns colors. She wants to make herself clear to her new appendage. She shakes so hard that even once she stands still, the world keeps tilting, fireworks keep bursting, her limbs stay unfamiliar to her, and when she lifts her dirty hands before her face, she does not recognize them. Her paddles, which have taken her to places she would never otherwise have seen, have disappeared. Her two great mitts! In their place she finds ten wiggling digits: slender and stretching and bumping into one another in their newness. How funny, Madeleine thinks, to go looking for a little knife, and then a nail, and to find instead, in the cool black soil, her fingers.

madeleine rejoices

I CAN BUTTON, SHE THINKS, and unbutton! I can light a match, hold a cigarette, and wave it languidly in the air. I can point at a person with whom I disagree. I can scratch a small itch. I am capable of pinching; also, of peeling an orange. I can take a photograph; remove a splinter; tuck a piece of hair behind my ear. I can be of help. I can grip, between my forefinger and my thumb, a penny nail. I can hang a curtain. I can build a riser. I can write, in tall red capitals, the letters of his name.

blessed

IT IS A MIRACLE. The full weight of it falls upon her. I am like Michel, she says aloud to the barn. In her cathedral, in her town, there is a picture of him in the window. Once, on a Sunday in summer, a blade of empyreal light illuminated his melancholy face, and she instantly recognized it as her own.

Why, it's me, she says to herself, full of wonder. I have been looking at myself all along.

For she has been restored, like the saint, to wholeness and perfection. Madeleine possesses two lips, two eyes, two arms, and now—ten immaculate fingers.

And the face will no longer be lengthened in sorrow, but bright and fluid with color. She will stand up from her family's pew and walk towards the stained glass, her eyes locked with her own. At the altar, she will pivot on her toes and face the congregation. Look upon me, she will say.

And even the devout will find it difficult to remember the suffering she has endured.

reprise

BUT THEN, STARING DOWN at her miraculous fingers, Madeleine remembers for what purpose they have been restored to her. Chastened, she corrects herself. She begins again:

The footlights will illuminate his once melancholy face. And the face will no longer be lengthened in sorrow, but bright and fluid with color.

Look upon me, he will say. I am Le Petomane.

And stepping out from the dark wings of the stage (the stage that is now in her power to build), Madeleine will pass through the audience (the audience that is helplessly attracted to her stage) as lightly as a breath of air. She will approach a stout man sitting in the front row, his brimless hat balanced on his knees, and she will touch his chest, with all the tenderness in the world. His stiff woolen vest will peel away like an orange rind, and she will graze her fingertips against the polished, orderly bones of his rib cage. Beneath, she will find a curled and pulsing bud, and when she blows on it, it will begin to unfurl its sanguine petals, one by one.

Gently touching with her newfound fingers, she will travel down each row of seats, and when she looks around she will notice, with pleasure, that the flowers she has uncovered are heliotropic, and that their delicate heads nod to M. Pujol wherever he goes, following his movements like those of the sun.

Stunned, sitting in an abandoned barn, her fingernails black with dirt, Madeleine imagines this: their hearts unfolding before him.

broken

MOTHER DISCOVERS that it is difficult to move. The fire has gone cold. The floor is unswept. The soft insides of pears have left sticky trails on her windows, and flies have come to congregate. But when she tries to rise from her seat, she cannot. She has only strength enough to turn her head slowly from side to side, observing the disrepair, how swiftly it has overtaken her house. Since when did crumbs litter the floor of her larder? Since when did that smell of spoilt milk fill the air?

It seems that she also has strength enough to clap. Children! she cries, clapping her hands. She hears a scuffling overhead; then a silence.

Children! she cries again, and finds that she is able to stamp her foot against the floor.

One by one they descend down the ladder, her scuffling children, her shamefaced children, who appear to have as much difficulty raising their heads as she does lifting herself from her chair.

Beatrice, she says. The fire.

Jean-Luc, she says. Help your father.

Lucie, she says. Wash the windows.

Claude, she says, to the child who is shuffling his feet the most miserably. Sweep the larder.

And to the youngest, to Mimi, she says, Bring me apples and pears.

But Maman, cries Mimi, before anyone can stop her: Nobody buys your preserves anymore.

It is true, a fact so plain that it must not be spoken. The children watch their mother in consternation. She is closing her eyes; she is nodding her head; she is accepting the truth of the remark. Collectively, the brothers and sisters wish for fury. But rather than inflaming her, the statement exhausts her, and she sinks, face slackening, back into her chair.

Silently, Mimi vows: I will fill a hundred baskets for her.

architect

MADELEINE MEASURES, placing one foot before the other. Here
will stand the proscenium. Here, the orchestra pit. And over there,
she would like for M. Pujol to have a private dressing room. But
with such luxuries, where will she put the seats? Red upholstered
seats, with armrests made of velveteen! She places one foot before
the other. She imagines the possibilities. She counts twenty-four,
twenty-five, twenty-six, and then her toe bumps into the wall. The
wall says: This is only a barn. Maybe a platform made of apple
crates, maybe a sheet hanging from the rafters, will have to do.

The walls of the barn are ribbed with light. From between the
planks, slats of daylight fall onto the floor, and as Madeleine
measures, she notices how they flicker, the narrow strips of light
beneath her feet. She puzzles over why that should happen, why
they should darken and then go bright again, as if each slim ribbon
were experiencing its own miniature eclipse, the moon passing in
rapid succession from one slat of light to the next. Why should such
a thing occur, Madeleine wonders, and with untimely delay the
answer arrives at the same moment she realizes: I am surrounded.

Or, more generally speaking, the barn is surrounded. By a
throng of onlookers, short in height, and long accustomed to
moving soundlessly. She feels their presence like a moist breath, the
air thickening with their shallow panting and their running noses,
with the effort it takes for them to stand still. Their faces press
against the cracks in the wall. Their knees and ankles itch in the
spiky grass. And she is not afraid, because they are only children.

What do you want? she says to the four walls.

Claude saw something, replies the farthest.

He said it made him feel strange, says a voice nearby.

We wanted to see it, too, says another.

Is he here? Madeleine asks, heart rising. Did he bring you?

She turns about in a circle, asking of the four walls, Claude?

Oh no, explains the far wall: He's in trouble. They all are. They cannot leave their yard.

Madeleine fights disappointment. She says, So. Do you feel strange?

They take a moment to consider.

A little, says one.

Not as much as I had hoped, admits another.

I feel precisely the same! the far wall declares.

In that case, says Madeleine, you should make yourselves useful.

She strides over to the barn door. The children swiftly shadow her, rushing in from all sides like water circling towards a drain, and she throws open the door. They are ready to meet her; they stand at attention. So many of them, looking famished and eager, restless and sly, capable of enormous secrets. They look exactly like the children she remembers.

The following, Madeleine says, are things that I need.

volunteer

AT THE HOSPITAL at Maréville, the flatulent man moves his finger lightly over the anatomical diagrams, noting: They will open me here. And here. They will make their way past the duodenum. The twisting jejunum. And then my gifts will be exposed!

A shadow passes over the page. M. Pujol looks up from his diagrams and sees that an enormous woman with very small wings is hovering outside the window and obscuring the light. He stands and raps upon the pane.

Madame, he says. I must beg you to move.

One moment! One moment! the woman gasps.

She shakes at him a handful of broadsheets: I have agreed to distribute these!

With a little kick against the window, the woman pushes off, and agitating her wings, maneuvers herself until she is hanging directly above the walled garden. Here, the hospital's inmates are taking their daily exercise. The matron marches in their midst, instructing them to lift their faces to the sunlight, to inhale deeply the smell of daffodils. The patients would very much like an excuse to lie down in the grass and loll about. So when a flurry of paper comes floating down from above, and the matron begins excitedly blowing upon her whistle, the inmates take this opportunity to stretch out on their backs, cross their ankles, and examine at their leisure the curious broadsheets, just as a Parisian would idle in the park with his morning paper. But rather than reading the news of the day, they read about the arrival of an astonishing phenomenon.

They see, in tall red capitals, the letters of his name. They gaze at his picture: a man delicately parting the tails of his coat.

His light restored, M. Pujol takes up where he left off. His finger finds again its place on the elegant diagram. This display of seriousness prompts the director to pause in the doorway and smile. Never before has a patient demonstrated the same eagerness he himself feels when undertaking an operation. It touches him, strangely. And in order not to dampen the subject's enthusiasm, he has restrained himself from mentioning certain risks.

smooth

I HAVE LEFT THE HOSPITAL behind me, Adrien thinks, his gaze fixed on the horizon, but sure enough, like a little dog or a servant girl, a sheet of paper comes flying out from behind the hospital gates, as if trying to delay him. It catches against the back of his knees and, stuck there, rustles plaintively.

The photographer twists about, freeing the paper from behind his legs, and though it flutters in his grip, he manages to read its tall red letters. His face brightens. Oh yes! He squints at the trembling page. I knew there was something I had forgotten to do.

Show him the poster; persuade him to come.

He remembers her hot, small body next to his in the cot.

Her sticky hands. Her voice whispering. A poster. His name. The people in my town. What else had she said?

The two of you—

You wanted to be alone.

And the photographer's face goes suddenly smooth, with the same sharp swiftness that Mother snaps the bedcovers straight— all thoughts, all creases, banished. He crumples the paper into a ball and pushes it deep inside his pocket. He refastens his eyes on the road ahead.

I have left the hospital behind me, says Adrien to himself, again.

math

OF ALL THE THINGS that she can do with her fingers, what Madeleine enjoys most is counting on them. She also likes to use them while giving orders. For instance, she can put her index finger to very imperious purposes, such as when she points at a high-backed chair and says, Move it over *there*. Then she can hold up her fingers and count, nine chairs—plus a milking stool, a piano bench, a daybed—after which she loudly announces, We need thirty-six more.

The children have thrown themselves entirely into the spirit of the enterprise. Among the items that Madeleine counts are four curtain rods, two chests of drawers, seven candlesticks, a cuspidor and, unrequested, eight brittle teacups from Limoges. Perhaps refreshments should be served during the intermission. The more sensitive audience members might require it, weakened as they will be after laughing so helplessly at the feats performed onstage. After shouting, howling, writhing, staggering; and some will probably begin to suffocate.

Madeleine counts the number of tickets she must supply, then counts the little footlights that will illuminate the stage. But no matter how many times she figures it, one calculation continues to escape her. Girl, photographer, flatulent man. Any lesser number will not suffice. For she and the flatulent man are exquisitely shy, incapable of looking one another in the face. While she and the photographer are capable only of groping. And the two men, together, do not exist unless she is there to gaze on them. What does that leave her with? The intractable number three.

As she counts it once more on her fingers, she is comforted unexpectedly by the arrival of a wonderful thought. She holds her fingers up to the light.

restoration

I CAN STROKE, she thinks, with the tip of this finger, the soft hair growing on the back of his neck. I can do it so gently, she thinks to herself, he will not even know that he has been touched.

Excuse me? asks a scratchy voice at her elbow.

She looks down into a smudged face.

I think you dropped this.

The boy hands her a braided cord she had been holding, just a moment ago, with the intent of attaching it to the curtain. Taking it between her fingers, she tells him, Thank you.

He smiles hugely. But before she knows it, he has fallen down onto his knees and leapt back up again. He is handing her, once more, the braided cord.

Here, he says. You dropped this. A second time.

She reaches out to grasp the cord, but seems suddenly to change her mind. She tucks her hands behind her back. She says to him,

Why don't you hold it for me?

Which the boy is more than delighted to do.

remains

MOTHER HAS LOST a bridegroom, a business, and seen her heirlooms devoured by moths. But her thoughts are occupied with other losses. They visit her, one by one, at the table where she sits, like petitioners, those things that have been misplaced or neglected in the course of her schemes. The thread of a conversation: You are a woman of science, she had ventured, but how had Mme. Cochon replied? The ending of a story: so did that bloody woman ever find her lovely face? And also lost, the goodwill of her neighbors: I am far too busy! she had puffed herself up on many occasions and said.

Lost too, perhaps, the trust of her children.

As if in answer to her thoughts, her youngest daughter appears before her. Her face is streaked with dirt and tears. She is holding something heavy in her skirts, the cloth bunched in her hands, the hands pressed to her heart. With a cry, she lets go. Fruit comes tumbling down from her skirts and goes scudding across the floor. When an apple finds its way to Mother's foot, she leans down with a sigh and takes it.

It is misshapen; it yields to the touch. If she were to bite into it, the mouthful would be mealy and bitter. Looking across her floor, she sees that all the apples and pears are similarly afflicted: humpbacked, wormeaten, spoiling on one side.

I looked and I looked, Mimi whispers, and this is what I found.

impress

CHILDREN HEAVING, the curtain is hoisted up to the sky. It
spills down from the rafters like a waterfall. Madeleine gets lost
in it, fumbling in the darkness, adoring its density and its weight,
the dusty smell in her nose.

How radiant she will appear, when she finally steps through!
She will welcome them, arms wide, heart pealing like a bell. And
the gift she is bringing them—her breath quickens as she thinks of
it, quickens as she pictures their delight, their laughter, pink faces,
gratitude. Why, it's nothing, she will tell them, just a little gift
I thought you would enjoy, a little something I picked up in my
travels. . . .

They will never have seen anything like him before.

And how lucky, and worldly, and generous she will appear:
the impresario who has brought them such unusual pleasures.
That is my daughter, her mother will murmur, and her siblings
will push forward in their frenzy to be the first to kiss her. Why
did I not see it before? her mother will wonder. How well she
looks, how bravely and wisely she carries herself, how her
complexion has brightened and her figure filled out, how she
has, in short, grown into a beautiful woman. Right beneath my
nose!

Madeleine wishes that she could remain wrapped in this
curtain until her moment of unveiling, muffled in the darkness
of her dusty red cocoon. But there is still work to be done. The

ticket booth is listing; twelve seats are missing; the floorboards need to be secured to the stage. So much more to do! she declares, bending down to grasp a nail, and when she cannot close her stiffening fingers around it, she whispers to them, Not yet. Not yet.

in the wings

SMALL, DIRTY FEATHERS drift down onto Madeleine's upturned face. Far above her, Mme. Cochon is flapping valiantly.

Do you see him? Madeleine calls. Is he coming down the road?

Possibly, the fat woman says. He is tall?

Oh yes, says Madeleine. Quite tall.

And wearing a smock?

Oh yes, says Madeleine. All the patients at the hospital must wear them.

But he no longer wears a moustache?

The matron made him take it off.

And his shoulders sag when he walks?

His life, says Madeleine, has not been easy.

In the stately manner of a hot-air balloon, Mme. Cochon floats down from the sky. Her whole self seems to have swollen with her expanded responsibilities. She is not only in charge of publicity, and spotting Le Petomane from afar; her title as stage manager is now official, and among her several duties is welcoming the performer, brushing out his coat, preparing him for his splendid entrance, as Madeleine warms up the audience.

Your star approaches, the stage manager announces, rearranging her wings: He is headed for the barn. He is crossing over ditches and climbing over stiles, as if he already knew the way. As if he were drawn here, like a pigeon flying home.

Of course he is drawn here, Madeleine replies. I have built him a stage.

amiss

IN THE MORNING, when he wakes, the mayor reaches beneath his bed and fails to find his chamberpot. The captain of the gendarmes sits down to his breakfast, only to discover that he has no seat to sit upon. The chemist goes to wash his face, but cannot; goes to open the curtains, but cannot; goes to complain to his obliging daughter, and learns that she also is gone.

mistaken

THE DOOR IS POUNDED with such force, it sets the fruit jumping on the floor. Mother sadly heaves herself up from her chair at the table. Her petitioners have lost their patience, it seems, for now they are shoving and crowding at her door.

Without opening it, she asks, What do you want?

The pounding stops. Through the door, she can hear the visitors muttering among themselves.

We have come to speak with you about your daughter, says a tentative voice at last, and she can picture, quite clearly, the mayor tugging at the buttons on his coat.

We have been robbed! says another voice, more reedy and forlorn, as she sees the chemist's spectacles sliding down his nose.

She has gathered up our things, and our children! say a multitude of voices all at once. Those of her acquaintances and neighbors, her former customers, her sworn enemies, her shopkeepers and bureaucrats. How sharply their faces appear to her now: how terrified, and bereft.

So she takes a step backwards, opening the door, and bumps into an army of her children, who have crept down the ladder and come silently to her defense. Mother unfolds her arms and takes them in.

As you can tell, she says to the mob at her door, my daughters are accounted for.

It's not Beatrice we want, the voices cry.

Nor Lucie, nor Mimi, the horde despairs.

They are looking for Madeleine, her children whisper.
Madeleine?

Mother nearly laughs. How many times must she tell them?
She raises her voice to the crowd: Madeleine is sleeping!

And with a sweep of her hand, she ushers them in: the mayor,
the priest, the captain, the chemist, and all of the suspicious wives.
They stumble over the spoiling fruit that is strewn across the floor.
Pressing in on the bed, they examine the sleeper: who takes up
room; who attracts attention; who lies there, sighing voluptuously,
as Mother stands at the door in an attitude of immense vindication.

But Madame, says the chemist, in his apologetic voice. I believe
you are mistaken.

charlotte

MOTHER ELBOWS HER WAY to the bed. Nonsense! she is preparing
to say, and put the conceited chemist in his place, but just as she
is opening her mouth, just as she is about to bring him low, the
word refuses to come forth.

Instead she says, It's you.

It's you, she thinks and reaches out to touch the beautiful
woman, fast asleep in the bed where her daughter ought to be.
If only you were not sleeping, you could tell me: Did you find it?
Did you ever find your voice, your lovely face? Mother thinks,
I would like to know.

But already Beatrice is beside her, pulling her back and
murmuring in her ear, It's not my fault. I told her, No. But she
was so tired, she wouldn't listen.

And already the mayor is clearing his throat, the women are
massing, the captain is stamping the heels of his boots, when a
small, gruff voice is heard from below.

It is Emma, the mayor's youngest daughter, who is squeezing
him by the hand.

Papa, she says, you must hurry. If you want to have a good seat,
you must come to the barn *right now.*

audience

WHAT AN ACUTE PLEASURE IT IS, to be reunited with one's things. To see one's children sitting straight in their chairs, hair combed, and hands folded in their laps. What a pleasure it is, to nod to one's neighbors, find a spot near the aisle, and adjust oneself in the seat; to enjoy the dimming of lights, ushers disappearing, programs rustling, an old gentleman coughing, and the breathless heavenly feeling that yes, yes, it is all about to begin....

ahem

MADELEINE SPREADS HER ARMS.

Ladies and Gentlemen, it is with great pleasure that I introduce the phenomenal M. Pujol. Though known to me as a kind and modest man, tonight he will be presented to you in dazzling splendor, as the toast of Paris, as the darling of Algiers, as all the rage in Antwerp and Ghent—simply put, as Le Petomane.

But before we begin tonight's performance, I would be remiss if I did not warn you of certain medical hazards. Upon witnessing his amazing gifts you will, I promise, feel the unmistakable desire to laugh. You might also experience the following urges: to scream, to cry, to grip your neighbor's knee, to beat your head upon the floor, to tear your clothing into pieces and go rolling through the aisles. Do not, at any cost, resist these urges. To do so would be to jeopardize your nervous systems.

I say this with a full understanding of his powers. Those who have suppressed their natural responses, who have attempted to maintain a modicum of dignity, have suffered the terrible consequences. Cases of apoplexy, suffocation, paralysis, and amnesia have been widely reported at the scenes of his performances.

For these reasons I ask you to take a small precaution: You must open your hearts to him, ladies and gentlemen, or risk the utter destruction of your health. It is that simple, and that serious.

But you have waited long enough. I can see you leaning forward in your seats. With no further ado, I introduce to you my great friend, my guide, my heart's delight . . . Le Petomane!

star

AND SO THE CURTAIN is lifted.

On stage: a large basin of water; a candlestick sitting atop a stool; a length of tubing; and a tarnished little flute with six stops, in order that he may play 'Au clair de la lune.' Everything is ready for him, but the sad and pale-faced man has not appeared.

From behind her, Madeleine hears the sound of her stage manager grunting. There is a fluttering of wings, and then a man comes stumbling out into the lights, as if propelled against his will by a much greater force.

He has been stripped of his smock, as Madeleine instructed, and stuffed into a black evening coat, one pilfered from the mayor especially for the occasion. It appears, at one shoulder, that he has already burst a seam. And it appears that Mme. Cochon has tried to smooth the cowlicks in his hair, for the signs of her struggle are everywhere, tiny bits of down clinging to his lapels, as though he has come freshly from wringing the neck of a goose. Yet in his heavy fist he clutches not a bird, but a filthy string, which trails behind him, weighted down by the battered kite at its end. Faded now after months in the sun and the wind, the kite still carries a picture of his cranium.

As for his face, it wears the dismayed expression of someone who finds himself in the wrong production. He looks back over his shoulder beseechingly, as if Mme. Cochon might whisper his lines, or a tremendous piece of scenery might roll out and flatten him beneath its wheels. How did I end up here? his whole body asks, twitching in the footlights, longing to disappear.

Upon seeing Madeleine, however, he seems to remember what it is that he is supposed to do. His eyes brighten; he steps forward with courage; he drops the kite string and—like that—it falls away from him, his clumsiness and coarseness and bewilderment, it all falls away. Like that, his purpose is revealed. He must unbutton his breeches. He must guide the little girl by her hand. He must wrap her little fingers around his cock. But doing so, his eyes fill with tears. Great drops of water spill down the half-wit's cheeks. Taking the hands of the girl in his own, he weeps over them.

gift

WHAT HAPPENED *to your hands?* The question gathers at the
back of the barn and sweeps forward in a bitter gust of curiosity.
Murmuring, and clucking, and craning their necks, the audience
asks what the idiot does not have the strength of mind to say. I am
not tonight's attraction! the girl protests, though looking down at
her hands, she sees that her two great mitts have at last completed
their return.

What happened? surges up once more from the audience. She
is suddenly glad that the half-wit is there to keep her from falling.
Not wanting to look again at her hands, she turns boldly to the
audience: It's nothing! she cries.

And peering out at them, she discerns their faces: jealous
Sophie, who now wears her hair piled atop her head; the bald-pated
chemist, who used to slip her sweets behind his counter; the bashful
mayor, his youngest daughter perched neatly on his lap; and
Mother, Father, her brothers and sisters, among them the foolhardy
Mimi, whom Mother is barely restraining from running forward to
the stage. Mysteriously, these faces she remembers as so particular
are now almost indistinguishable to her, every one of them stricken,
every one of them wearing an identical look: of guilt, and most
especially of pity.

She cannot bear to be the object of this look.

But they have made me special! she insists. They have taken me
to places I would never otherwise have been.

And displaying her mangled hands for all to see, she repeats a phrase borrowed from M. Pujol: An abnormality, to be sure, but I consider it, as should you, a gift!

The audience remains unconvinced.

act

LOOK, SHE SAYS, I can tuck my feet behind my ears, and waddle about on my hands.

But when she demonstrates, the spectators simply shake their heads and sigh.

Listen, she says, disentangling herself, I can make a sound louder than a thunderclap!

But when she slams her mitts together, only the idiot jumps in surprise; the barn fills with the rustle of people shifting in their seats.

This I know you will like, she tries again. I can start the bullfrogs singing.

And blowing into the horn of her hands, she makes a deep, sad, bellowing sound, the lowest note in M. Pujol's scale, and soon enough, rising up in all directions, comes the distant chorus of frogs, jowls swelling with song, their voices carrying from all the wet corners of the world: the riverbank, the millpond, the water hole behind the barn, the empty pool where a widow once kept her fish.

The audience finds this stirring performance merely cause for greater pity. Madeleine hears the sound of sniffling, and is enraged.

Among the rich, she shouts, my gifts are in great demand!

encore

THE HALF-WIT HAS already unbuttoned his breeches. So it is with little difficulty that she arranges him: he must arch his back; he must let his head drop between his arms; he must appear more dog-like. In exasperation, Madeleine presses her hand into the small of M. Jouy's back: Like so!

There once was a widow, she shouts at the barn, who so favored my talents, she would say of them only, Louder!

And, *smack!* is the sound of a girl's hand falling squarely upon the backside of an idiot. *Smack!* is the sound of her palm meeting the flesh of his bared cheeks.

She lived in a very grand house, Madeleine cries. She had Persian carpets in every room. But nothing gave her greater pleasure than the sight of my two hands!

And once again she displays them proudly, as if they are a hundred times more rare than anything this barn has ever seen. In truth, Madeleine is sorry to have them back in her possession. She is sorry never to have stroked the hair on M. Pujol's neck, and she would have liked to touch the pulsing hearts of her neighbors; in truth, the short life of her ten perfect fingers is causing her own heart to wither, and it is all she can do to keep from weeping stupidly as the half-wit—but she would rather die than show regret, so she brings her paddle down more swiftly on the idiot.

There once was a man, she declares, who had suffered so much, he found relief, he found solace, in the touch of these hands.

But the person whom she is paddling now does not shiver and moan as M. Pujol once did. Instead he is making a snuffling noise; he is choking, it seems, on the spill of his tears.

If only you knew Le Petomane, she tells the audience. If only he were here.

inevitable

IN UTTERING THESE WORDS, she sees him at last, M. Pujol. He is
not nearing the barn, nor mounting the stage she has built for him.
Nor is he naming the parts of his body, as he trembles beneath the
photographer's brave hands. M. Pujol is sleeping: a patient etherized
upon a table. The director is quaking slightly in his excitement. He
presses the tip of his scalpel against the pale skin, then retreats; he
presses again, and draws back his hand. Too quickly, it will all be
over; and he would like the anticipation to last forever.

As for Adrien, the photographer, he is miles away from the
hospital at Maréville. His little wagon of photographic equipment
still rattles in his wake. He has traveled for many days, he has
wandered into a market, and, stumbling over a mangy dog, he has
found a stall selling figs—and though he tests the fruit between his
fingers, he refuses to think of what he has forgotten to bring with
him. Now he is standing in the center of Paris, on the boulevard des
Capucines, ringing at the door of his brother. He presses against the
bell and listens; he pushes it several times in quick succession, and
strains to hear the sound of footsteps on the stair; he leans upon it
with his entire weight, but cannot detect any movement, any sign
of life, inside.

Madeleine, she is beating on an idiot: a decent, speechless,
lumbering man who had once tucked pennies in her pockets. She
lifts her hand, and lets it fall; she repeats the gesture helplessly, again
and again.

exit

SEEING AT LAST THE THREE OF THEM—girl, photographer, flatulent man—caught forever thus, and thus forsaken, she thinks, What terrible things we do, in our efforts to be admired.

And it is with unthinkable strain that she resists the weight of her paddle, the pull of the earth, the stunned gaze of the audience and, most heavy, her wounded pride; it is with every inch of her being that she keeps her hand from falling upon the backside of M. Jouy.

But the flatulent man, and Adrien—what can she do to stop them? What can she possibly do? To lift the knife from his skin, to lift his finger from the bell . . .

Indeed, there is very little she can do. She can neither button nor unbutton. She cannot open a tin of cigarettes, count to ten, wear a ring. Divertissements on the piano, or intricate needlework, or the pretty handwriting that one sees on invitations—all are impossible for her. As is keeping a clean house, slicing vegetables, mending holes in socks and fences, safeguarding neatness and order. Confusion will accompany her, always. And she will never build a single thing again, most especially a stage. Even with these uncanny hands, she has failed them, her audience.

Stealing a look at their worried faces—Sophie, Emma, the chemist, the mayor, her brothers and sisters, grown so tall, and then, most worn, most loving, the face most known and feared, her Mother!—she drops down upon the stage, stretches out along the floorboards, and closes her eyes.

she dreams

CHARLOTTE AWAKES in an unknown house, in an unknown bed, and wearing someone else's clothes. Sliding out from the covers, she feels the unfamiliar floor beneath her feet, and finds her balance by placing her palm on a table she has never seen. The window, the tree outside it, the bird singing in the branches of the tree. Even the smell of her own skin is foreign: pungent, and dark, and reminiscent of wine.

The kitchen she wanders through is deserted, the chairs in disarray, but the fire is still smoking, and the pot still warm. What is inside the pot she cannot tell; she lifts the lid and sniffs, takes a spoon from the table and stirs. I will have to try it, she decides, but the taste in her mouth is neither savory nor sweet; it tastes somewhat of apples but also of lamb.

And entering the yard she sees that it, too, has been abandoned, though only minutes ago, for the grass is still trampled underfoot and the cows in the pasture are lowing. From the empty yard, she passes through the garden and into the overgrown orchard.

She is not surprised when she fails to recognize the fruit: discolored, misshapen, not quite resembling one kind or another. But it is here, in the orchard, that she sees at last a thing that is familiar to her, leaning up against a tree, as if having waited a lifetime for her to appear. Charlotte takes it in her arms, sits down on a stump, and, embracing it between her legs, begins to play.

conversion

MARGUERITE, UPON the desertion of so many of her entertainers, has fallen back on her own devices. Every night, after all, there is still the widow leaning forward in her chair, expecting pleasure. What is Marguerite to do but unlock her monstrous trunk, exhaling clouds of musk, and shake out her ancient costumes? The general's uniform, the lover's red cape, the burnished breastplate worn by a vengeful son. She also digs up, from the very bottom, her sword, which she slices through the air with untrammeled delight.

Of course, she must remember how to walk. How to swing her arms, and beat her chest, and meet a comrade heartily. That is easy enough to master. More tedious is wrestling her bosom back into its old restraints, tugging on the powdered wigs; the effort is proven worthwhile, however, upon her discovery that thus disguised, she has managed to enchant the restless widow. She finds an amorous note slipped beneath her door. She finds herself the object of winks, and eloquent glances. In the mornings, when she steps out from her caravan, she is greeted by an avalanche of roses.

Who is Marguerite, not to welcome love when it arrives at last? Wearing her red cape and brandishing her sword, she courts the widow; she wins her hand; she takes up residence in the very grand house, and learns that if one concentrates, growing a William II moustache is not so difficult to do.

nocturne

A FISHING VILLAGE sits at the edge of a warm sea. The moon beats her path across the waves, across the little boats rocking in their moors, past the shuttered shops and dark cafés, up a flight of whitewashed stairs, and through the open window of a rented apartment. Alighting upon an empty basket beneath the sill, and then a bottle, also empty, the moon comes tumbling into the room. She illuminates a chair, over which is draped an elegant tailcoat, a white butterfly tie, a pair of black satin breeches. She uncovers a wagon, inside of which is gathered a small family of flutes. And gliding up to the rumpled expanse of the bed, she finds what she has been searching for: a head resting on another's chest, his pale face loosened in sleep. He breathes deeply. He does not moan. His head rises and falls with the other's inhalations, and the movement is as gentle, as infinite, as that of a fishing boat lulled by the sea.

Shyly the moon extends her white fingers. She caresses the two men dreaming in the bed. Her hands are so light, and so full of care, that when they awake, they will not even know that they have been touched.

stirring

MADELEINE STIRS in her sleep.

stain

THE BARN IS SILENT. All eyes are fixed upon the sleeping girl. She lies there, indifferent to their gaze: inert, dreaming, blank, detached. Innocence, some might take it for, the audience seeing her as if for the first time, as if she has been restored, through sleep, to her proper dimensions; she is only a girl, asleep, her hands folded neatly on her chest. She looks small. Her monstrous hands look small as well. The people of her town cannot stop gazing at them, at how quietly they lie. They watch her hands with the absorption of a poet, who cannot bear to look away from his mark on the page, the word he has left there.

hush

FROM BEHIND the curtain comes a fluttering, and Mme. Cochon steps out onto the stage. Her hair is dishevelled, her wings are askew, but it is with a beautiful degree of poise that she extracts her diary from deep between her breasts. When she opens the book, its pages fan out like a peacock's tail. The audience sighs at this disturbance, as if she were a noisy member in their midst. But she will not be silenced. She says to them:

You know me as a woman of science. For months you have seen me at work on this volume, in which I've recorded many small and mysterious signs. Now, at last, I wish to share with you my findings.

Holding her book in one hand, gathering up her fat in the other, Mme. Cochon sweeps past the half-wit, and like a dainty lady forced to navigate a puddle, she frowns at the girl lying asleep on the stage, and finally steps over her, as though she were of little matter.

From the first page of her book, the woman reads:

Hush.

And together, the neighbors, the brothers and sisters, together they inhale softly and the barn fills with one endless exhalation of breath: Shhhhhhhhhhhhh.

It is all about to begin.

notes

GRATEFUL ACKNOWLEDGMENT is made to the following authors and works: Roland Barthes, *Camera Lucida* (New York, 1981); Ludwig Bemelmans, *Madeline and the Gypsies* (New York, 1959); George Eliot, *Middlemarch* (London, 1872); Yasunari Kawabata, *House of the Sleeping Beauties and Other Stories* (New York, 1969); Jean Nohain and F. Caradec, *Le Petomane 1857–1945* (Los Angeles, 1967); Andrew Porter, liner notes from *Handel: Arias for Durastanti* (Los Angeles, 1992); Sir Bart Sacheverell Sitwell, *Baroque and Rococo* (New York, 1967).